Hollywood Dreams

A HOLLYWOOD HOPEFUL NOVEL

MOLLY O'HARE

Dedication

This story is dedicated to anyone who was ever told they were not good enough.
Anyone who felt their size, personality, or demeanor has been looked down upon.
This novel goes out to you.
And honestly, look anyone in the face that says you are not good enough and after you mentally throat punch them (I'm not telling you to actually do it... Please don't go to jail) tell them to eff off and say, "watch me!" Rock who you are, and even though it can be hard sometimes, find something to love about yourself each and every day!

Hollywood Dreams

A HOLLYWOOD HOPEFUL NOVEL

MOLLY O'HARE

Chapter One

MAGGIE CONNOLLY SAT in her beat-up, piece-of-shit old car, trying to get her nerves under control. Two weeks shy of her twenty-seventh birthday, she finally felt like she was getting somewhere in her career.

She was going to be in a movie!

Although, if you were to ask Maggie's mother, Nancy, it'd be a different story. It was her mother's favorite pastime to tell Maggie she'd never make it and to move back home. She relished in it. The gene parents were *supposed* to have to encourage their children somehow skipped Maggie's mother entirely.

That wouldn't stop Maggie, though. Nope, she was not going to let her mother or anyone from back home in Florida try and crush her dreams.

Not this time. Not ever.

Maggie dreamed of being an actor. She ate, slept, and breathed acting.

Even when everyone told her she couldn't be a film star, she didn't care. This was her destiny and anyone that didn't believe that could go fuck themselves.

So what if she had twenty or thirty extra pounds that would never go away? Why did it matter if her hair is more brown than blonde? Who cares if she cursed a little more rampantly than the next person?

If it didn't matter to her, why should it matter to anyone else?

Acting was in her blood, and she would stop at nothing to accomplish her dreams. Anyone that thought any different could screw themselves.

As Maggie sat in her car, she thought back on the past couple of years. She'd been cast here and there, but never for a lead role or anything substantial. She still managed to acquire a decent résumé. If you were to ask her, she'd tell you, she was the best, "Mmm Good," soup commercial actor there ever was.

Regardless, no matter how hard she tried she never seemed to break into the spotlight.

The worst part was, she knew the reason why. It had nothing to do with her talent. Nope. Her talent was only secondary to one thing.

She'd had her fair share of casting directors inform her exactly what was wrong with her. She didn't look the part. She wasn't what they pictured. She'd even been told her look wasn't "Hollywood" enough. Whatever the hell that was supposed to mean.

Assholes.

One casting director had the nerve to tell her she should look into *Voice Acting*. His words: "Honey, you don't have a face for film. You're not who women want to be, and you're not who men want to be with. You might as well cut your losses. Go back home and open a restaurant or something."

Open a restaurant?

And the worst part was he was dead serious. Dead freaking serious.

Open a freaking restaurant. Just because someone had a few extra pounds does not mean they'd be restaurant material. Seriously, what the fuck? Maybe that casting director should open a poop factory with all the shit pouring out of his mouth if we were going by his logic.

Besides, if it wasn't for the fact that Maggie couldn't cook or handle finances, she still couldn't see herself abandoning her dream. No matter how many people told her to.

Instead, Maggie took that criticism and turned it into drive.

Never the one to miss an opportunity though, Maggie might have also printed out a picture of the casting director and used his face as her new dart board, but that was beside the point.

Sadly, that type of treatment wasn't anything new to her. She'd been picked on her whole life, for everything. Even her own mother didn't believe in her.

Maggie wasn't going to let any of that stop her. It didn't matter if she didn't look "Hollywood," she was as good, if not better than her peers.

And, she could prove it.

Sit her in front of the camera and bam, she became another person. When Maggie was in front of the camera, she came alive. That's how she knew she was going in the right direction.

In the end, Maggie told everyone who belittled her to *fuck off*. She then moved clear across the country to California in pursuit of her dreams.

And right now, Maggie had been in California going on three months with nothing to show for it. But, she wasn't going to let that stop her. If she were being honest, at this point she was really missing those soup commercials.

It was the same thing every day. Get up, try to make yourself look "Hollywood," whatever the hell that meant, and go on auditions. Go back home, eat, sleep, repeat.

One week, no callbacks.

Two weeks, no callbacks.

Three weeks, still no callbacks.

Was she going to let that stop her? Hell no. She wasn't going to pack her bags and run back home with her tail between her legs. No, Maggie Connolly was going to keep on fighting, rejection and all.

And that persistence led her to right now.

After weeks of trying, Maggie finally got her first part. It wasn't anything significant. Heck, it was probably no more than thirty seconds of screen time. But damn, it made her proud. That part was hers and she was going to own it like it was her big Hollywood break.

Her, Maggie Connolly, was cast in her first role in a real-life Hollywood production.

"Take that, Momma!" Maggie had yelled once she got off the call with her agent. She knew this was just the start.

Coming back to the present, Maggie took a deep breath before she opened her car door.

She'd tried to follow the directions to get to the correct soundstage. But, unfortunately for her, there'd been construction on the lot forcing her to make some unexpected detours.

After thirty minutes of screaming, crying, and yelling to the sky that, "the universe hated her and must be in cahoots with her mother," she was finally parked in front of Soundstage 1B.

Maggie stepped out of her car and couldn't stop herself from doing a little jig. She still couldn't believe it. She was going to be working on Hollywood's most anticipated summer movie.

Hell freakin' yeah!

Everyone was talking about the action-adventure romance, starring none other than Hollywood's *it* boy, Trevor McCain.

Trevor McCain. Maggie sighed, thinking of him.

He was everything you thought of when you heard Hollywood leading man. He had chiseled good looks that models strived for, that alpha male persona, *and* the reputation to back it up. He was *the* bad boy in and out of the movies. Hell, he was voted number four on the most attractive men list published last year.

Although, in Maggie's opinion, Trevor should have won. He had chestnut hair that begged to have hands run through it and deep blue eyes that could bring you to your knees. And let's not forget his body... Man, his body was something else. Maggie had to fan herself when she thought of it.

The definition of his abs... Whoa, momma! You know that 'v' that makes women drool? He had that tenfold.

In his last movie, he'd done a love scene that still had Maggie weak in the knees. That man could melt ice on a cold day in the North Pole.

There was no denying Trevor McCain was Maggie's Hollywood crush.

Her, along with half of the world's population, chose him to be their dream man. And she was about to be in a movie with him, even if it was just a small role.

She could scream, dance, and jump for joy. Here she was, chubby, plain Jane, or plain Maggie, as she liked to call it, going to work alongside Trevor McCain.

Trevor. Freaking. McCain!

Well, maybe not alongside him, but at least in the same movie, right? She didn't care. She was over the freakin' moon about it.

Maggie looked down at the script in her hand as a broad smile spread across her face. This was her time to shine.

She'd had it for a few days now. Sadly, Trevor's character wasn't in the scene. She'd be lucky if he were even on set today.

Man, the possibility to get just a glimpse of him in real life sent shivers down her body. She'd love to see his perfectly tight ass in the flesh.

I wonder if I'd be able to bounce a quarter off of it? She shivered. *Yeah, it could totally be done.*

Then again... Maybe not seeing Trevor was a good thing. With her luck, she'd get all tongue-tied, end up forgetting her lines and make a fool out of herself in front of him.

Ugh. Then there was the horror of her fantasy Trevor being better than the real Trevor.

Let's keep fantasy Trevor up on that pedestal.

Yeah, that was a better plan. Not seeing him at all was a good thing.

As Maggie stood alongside her car, she realized there was a problem. She was lost. As in no freaking clue where she was.

Her first time on a *real* set and it was already a mess. She looked down at her watch as panic crept through her. Call time was approaching and she hadn't even figured out how to get into the building.

Maggie took a deep breath. "Okay, Mags. You can do this."

Maggie hiked her backpack onto her shoulder and walked over to the building. And it was just her luck the first door she tried was locked. Same as door two.

"No big deal," she remarked. "Happens all the time." She pushed her bag higher on her shoulder and moved to the other door further down. Thankfully, the third one she tried opened. When she walked inside, she felt the cool breeze from the air-conditioning hit her face. "See, everything is fine. No need to panic."

She looked at the call sheet in her hand telling her where she needed to go first. There was a map on the back, but she couldn't tell which way the map was facing. She flipped it around a couple of times before she closed her eyes.

This is it, Mags. You are finally doing what you love to do, what you are meant to do. Don't let this little blip screw with your mojo. You're Maggie Connolly, strong, funny, and fierce. There is no one like you, and you have something to give. She opened her eyes.

Maggie started walking down the hall and stopped when she came to the first door. Maybe if she were lucky, there would be someone inside who'd point her in the right direction.

She opened the door and immediately froze. *Holy crapolie!*

"Harder, Trevor! Fuck me harder!"

Oh God, oh God, oh God! Maggie's eyes widened as she realized what she'd walked into. In an instant, it was as if her life flashed before her eyes. *Really, Universe? Just one more thing, right? This is exactly what I needed to see!*

Before Maggie could do anything, the door she'd pushed open, hit the wall loud enough to have the otherwise occupied couple turn her way.

"I'm sorry!" Maggie screamed in a panic. She could feel the tears in her eyes. How could this morning get any worse? She reached for the handle to pull the door shut but was stopped when she heard his bellowed voice.

"Who the fuck are you?" Trevor growled, pushing the blonde off. "Why the hell are you even in this room?"

"I-I," Maggie stuttered, once again frozen. *Today must be the 'screw with Maggie Connolly day!'*

"I *said* who the fuck are you?" he spat, pulling up his pants. "Let me guess, you're some snot-nose little intern, or are you here to snap a pic or get a recording to sell to the tabloids?" He narrowed his eyes at her, his lips going thin.

Sure, Maggie had seen him angry in films, but never like this.

"What?" Maggie finally found her voice, before turning slightly. She couldn't stare at his naked chest while it was covered with sweat. She felt the heat in her cheeks as the embarrassment of the situation set in.

"Answer me," he snapped. "Fuck it! I'll call security so they can escort your sorry ass off the lot."

"No," Maggie replied. "It was just a mistake. I was trying to find the area I needed to check-in at. I wasn't trying to spy on you. Whatever you mean by that. I'm just here to film my part."

Trevor stared at her, his face cold, his eyes dark. "You?" He looked her up and down. "You're here to film a scene? What, does the Pillsbury Dough Boy need a replacement?"

Maggie shook her head trying to will away the tears. Normally, she'd be the first to call out his remark, but with the morning she'd had and the fact that her dream man, with only nine words, crushed everything inside of her, Maggie's brain wouldn't function.

"More like Quasimodo or maybe a stand-in for a pig." The blonde woman laughed.

Maggie yanked the door shut and took off down the hall. She wasn't looking, so it wasn't a surprise when she ended up running right into someone.

"Whoa there! You okay? Need some help?"

Maggie looked up to see who she'd plowed into. She didn't know his name, but she recognized him from the audition. He was around her age, maybe a little older.

"It's Maggie, right?" he asked as he smiled warmly at her.

She nodded, still trying to gather her composure. Not only was she just humiliated by her Hollywood crush, but she ended up running headfirst into someone who'd cast her.

Screw you, Universe and all the universe-y things you do!

"What's got you all upset there, Maggie?" He moved a piece of her hair behind her ear.

"I just got lost," she replied, trying to get her breathing under control. She'd already made a fool out of herself once, no need to do it again.

"The construction?" He rolled his eyes. "It happened to all of the actors today. There was supposed to be an email sent out with alternate routes once you got on the lot. Trust me, you're not the only one who is having a hard time." His smile morphed into a big toothy grin. "That's why I'm headed to the lot to see if I can help round up the other actors." He made a motion like he was throwing a lasso which made her laugh.

"Thank you. Sorry I almost knocked you down." She bit her bottom lip.

"No thanks needed, Maggie." He held out his hand for her to shake. "I'm Danny Erikson."

She cocked her head to the side as the name dawned on her. "As in Danny Erikson, the son of Matthew Erikson, the director?"

"That would be the one." He nodded with a smile.

"Oh shit." She blanched as she placed her head in her hands defeated. "Can today get any worse? First, I get lost then I'm accused of being some sort of spy and now I've run over the director's son." Her shoulders slumped. "If you could just point me in the direction of where my car should be, I'll go ahead and see myself out."

"What are you talking about?" Danny asked, stopping her. "Do you not want the part anymore?"

Was he serious? Maggie cocked her brow at him.

"You know," he started. "My dad and I talked about your audition that afternoon." The right side of his mouth turned up in a grin. "You had us in stitches. You're funny, Maggie, and very talented."

Maggie knew she was staring at him like he had two heads. "I, um—"

Just then she heard a door from where she'd just come from slam. *Shit!*

She knew exactly what that was. She then heard the distant voice of none other than Trevor McCain.

Maggie quickly shot her attention back to Danny. "Yes, Mr. Erikson, I still want the part. Can you show me where I need to go?" she hurried out, hoping to get the show on the road before all hell broke loose.

"Danny," he corrected. "Please call me Danny. Sure, let me show you where you gotta go." Danny placed his hand on the small of her back, moving her through the halls. When they made it to the green room, she was thankful not to see any sign of Trevor *or* the blonde.

Maggie didn't want to bail on her first film here in LA, but she *definitely* did not want to run into them again. Maggie needed to come up with a plan. If she could figure out a way to hide long enough to avoid them both, she should be able to do her scene and leave with no one being the wiser.

A plan had to work, right? The Universe wouldn't screw with someone that many times in one day, would it?

Yeah. She'd be fine. This would work.

While Maggie was getting her hair and makeup done, she thought back to the way Trevor treated her. This was the exact reason she never wanted to meet actors she liked. There was no way in hell she'd ever be able to see him any other way than a fucktwad. Albeit a hot fucktwad, but still, a fucktwad.

He didn't have to treat her that way.

Fuck him! Hopefully, that blonde gave him gonorrhea.

Taking a deep breath, Maggie shook it off. There was no need to dwell on it right now anyway.

It wasn't like it was the first time someone said hurtful things to her. And, it most certainly wasn't going to be the last.

Plus, the likelihood of seeing him again was slim to none.

Chapter Two

TREVOR WATCHED as the door slammed shut. He was so fucking over it. Every time he turned a corner, there was someone trying to snap a picture of him to sell to the highest bidder. This wasn't the first time they'd tried to catch him hooking up with someone.

He was beyond over it. It never fucking ended. So, when he saw the tears in the eyes of the chick that ran out, he wanted to pat himself on the back.

Sure, he lived his life like he was going to die tomorrow and everyone wanted to know who he was sleeping with next, but that gave them no right to invade his privacy.

Trevor growled out his annoyance.

She could have at least come up with a better excuse. Being here to film? Yeah right. *And, pigs are gonna fly out of my ass.*

Trevor looked at Cassie, at least that's what he thought her name was. He'd only met her an hour ago. She was decent enough. She had huge tits and an even bigger ass. Her voice was annoying but he could overlook that for a few hours. But after the intrusion, he was done.

"Get dressed, Cassie," he growled, as he tossed her shirt toward her.

"Why?" Instead of putting it on, she looked at him with a devilish smile on her face. "I doubt she'll be coming back. You saw the way she left here, right? I'm pretty sure she'll never step foot on this soundstage again," she remarked, joyfully.

Cassie had a point, but it didn't matter. He'd already lost his stiffy, and he didn't see it coming back anytime soon. Plus, the more Cassie talked the more his dick wanted to hide.

"I can't believe she said she was here to film. Did you get a look at her? Eww. No wonder you're going soft." Cassie laughed.

Her voice was now like nails against a chalkboard. *Fuck this shit.* He didn't have time for this, plus he had shit to do now.

Trevor looked at the door with narrowed eyes. He was going to find that chick and make sure her ass was kicked off the set. He turned back to Cassie, now on a mission. "Get dressed. We're done."

After searching for about thirty minutes and not finding her, Trevor gave up. She was probably long gone by now anyway.

"Trevor?"

He turned to see Danny walking his way. Trevor did his best to stifle his growl of annoyance. This kid was a piece of work. It was people like Danny that annoyed him the most. A complete "yes-man".

And Trevor could prove it. He'd ask Danny for the stupidest things just to see if the dumbass would actually go and get it. He always did, without fail.

As a wicked smile appeared on his face he wondered if he asked for a glass of water with exactly eight ice cubes, shaped like dicks if this kid would actually go and hunt it down for him.

He gave Danny the once-over. Yup, he would do it. There was no doubt in his mind he did whatever anyone asked of him.

Trevor had zero respect for the kid. Danny was clearly riding on his father's coattails. Which was kind of sad for his age. He was pretty sure Danny was only a few years younger than him.

"I didn't know you were on set today?" Danny cocked his head to the side as she looked at him.

"When I talked to Matt yesterday, we decided I should come in. We might have time to rework some solo scenes."

"Gotcha." Danny shrugged. "I believe they're finishing up the table read and will be starting soon. Is there anything I can get you?"

Trevor contemplated asking for the water with the dick ice in it but decided against it. With his luck, before he took his first sip there would be rumors floating around. He moved past him. "No. I'm gonna go to my trailer. Tell your dad I'll come to the set in about an hour."

"Ten-four," Danny agreed. "We should still be filming the first bar scene then. I know he wanted to try for a few different angles that weren't on the call sheet."

Ignoring Danny, Trevor started walking through the soundstage to his trailer. He kept scanning his surroundings.

There was no sign of her anywhere.

Good.

"I CAN DO THIS," Maggie whispered as she walked onto the set.

This was going to be her big chance. Well, not her make it or break it moment. She wasn't expecting to be discovered with her little scene. But it was going to be her first time in a real movie.

And damn it, that was a big deal.

"There you are," Danny remarked the moment she stepped onto the soundstage. "We're just about ready for ya." He sent her another welcoming smile.

"Awesome." Maggie's face lit. She really liked Danny, the energy that came off of him was contagious.

"Good to see you again, Maggie," Matt Erikson, the director, commented as he made his way from behind a façade.

"Likewise." She nodded.

"Okay, guys and gals," Matt announced, addressing the crew. "Basically, in this scene, you're the waitress taking the drink orders." He looked at Maggie. "They're gonna give you a hard time, use that when you deliver your lines. You hate your job. When you bring back the drinks, one of the guys is gonna grab you, all you have to do is throw the drink in his face. Sound good?"

"Sure," Maggie answered. She couldn't help the retort that came next, "Be a bitch, hate everyone, then throw a drink in someone's face. I do that every day," she joked. "This is gonna be a piece of cake."

Matt and Danny both laughed. "See Dad, told you she was perfect for this."

Maggie couldn't help but beam. She really liked Danny. Not only did he make her feel better, but he genuinely seemed like a good person. Maybe, after this, they could be friends.

Lord knew she needed friends. She hadn't made a single one since moving to California.

Thankfully, she hadn't needed a roommate. When Maggie's grandmother passed away, she'd left her a nice inheritance to follow her dreams. She was the only one that had ever believed in her.

Pushing the thoughts away, she looked at Danny. *Maybe Danny could end up being my first friend here?*

"Come on, Maggie," Danny said, touching her elbow. "I'll show you to your first mark."

A few hours later, Maggie was over the moon. Everything had gone super well. They'd been able to film the scene multiple times. The crew was able to get some great action takes. And, she'd tell anyone that asked, the best part way by *far* being able to toss the drink into the guy's face.

Each time she did it, it got better and better. It might have also got out a bit of frustration too, but she'd never admit to that.

They were just about to shoot the scene again but at an "over the shoulder" frame when she heard it.

"What the fuck is she doing here?"

Maggie's whole body jerked in panic as she quickly turned to the noise only to see Trevor McCain stomping onto the set. She felt the color drain from her face as her stomach bottomed out to the floor.

Oh, crap!

"What's going on?" Matt asked, looking at Trevor.

Matt looked pissed. *Good. Maybe he'd kick Trevor off the set before all hell broke loose. Yeah, and maybe if I bent over pigs would fly out of my ass.*

"That bitch..." Trevor pointed right at Maggie. "Needs to be escorted off the set right now," he growled.

"I'm sure this is all just a misunderstanding," Danny chimed in, trying to defuse the situation.

"Misunderstanding my ass." Trevor walked right in front of Maggie, towering over her. "She snuck into one of my private rooms and tried to take a picture of me in a *compromising* position."

"What?" Maggie shook her head. "That's not what happened."

Trevor glared down at her. "Yes, it is," he said. "She waited outside the door for her moment and pounced when the timing was right."

"That's not true!" she yelled. *Could today get any worse?*

"Really?" Trevor snapped. "Do you deny walking in the room?"

"N-n-no," Maggie stammered. When she saw a triumphant smile appear on his face she quickly added, "I was lost and somehow got turned around. I only opened the door *hoping* it was the right place for me to go."

"Yeah right." Trevor rolled his eyes. "Try a more believable lie." He looked her up and down. "I must say I'm pretty surprised you *are* actually here for a part, though."

Maggie could feel the embarrassment of his earlier words come back. "I really—"

"Who the fuck cast her?" he cut her off.

"Trevor," Matt remarked somewhat close to the tone of voice you would use to calm an out of control animal. "I'm sure we can get this worked out."

"No. I want to know." He looked back at her. "Why in the hell would anyone cast someone that looked like *her* as a waitress in a bar? The waitress needs to be hot, not..." He pointed his finger at her, looking up and down. "...that."

Screw this!

Maggie already knew the chances of them keeping her on set were slim to none. And right now, she didn't give a flying fuck.

This was her last straw.

Before she knew it, Maggie felt all the rage from the negative words from her mother, all of the rejections she'd gotten, the casting directors that picked her apart. And all the horrible, uncalled for things *him* and that blonde bitch said to her.

And now, in front of everyone, she was once again being cast off as the ugly, no-good loser.

Something snapped inside of her.

Not this time! Not. Fucking. This. Time. She narrowed her eyes. *Okay, Universe, you wanna play? I'll play.*

Maggie clenched the glass in her hand as she walked behind Trevor. "Excuse me?" she said, disgust dripping from her words.

"Quiet, little girl, the grownups are talking."

"Really?" she spat before looking around. "I hope to God you don't count yourself as a grownup in this?"

Trevor turned toward her about to say something when she stopped him. "I don't know why everyone is so fascinated with you. Yeah sure, you've got a hot body, but the way you treat people is repulsive. You act like a spoiled two-year-old that was just told he needed to take a Goddamn nap."

Trevor's lips thinned as his eyes pierced into her.

"And, another thing!" she continued. "If you are going to screw someone and you *don't* wanna get caught, lock the fucking door, you moron. If you're so concerned..." She used air quotes. "...about someone coming in to snap a picture of your little willy to sell it to the tabloids, you'd think you'd be more proactive and *lock the fucking door.*" Maggie's breathing increased as the weight of everything crashed into her all at once.

"Maggie," Danny tried to interrupt.

"Just because you're a star does not give you the right to tear people down. You think it makes you look cool to tell everyone I don't *fit* the role? Does it make your overinflated ego feel better to tear me down?" She took a step closer to him. "Well, fuck you! Fuck you and the no-good piece of shit horse you rode in on. You're pathetic!" She turned to walk away but instead looked over her shoulder at him. "I hope that bitch gave you chlamydia!"

Gasps and laughter echoed through the room as everyone on set reacted to her words.

She stood a little taller as she puffed out her chest. *That's right, come at me. I am Maggie hear me roar.* Taking a deep breath, she walked over to the table and grabbed her tray ready to get back into position.

She felt someone touch her shoulder. "Ma'am?"

Maggie looked behind her and saw a security officer. "Don't bother," she snapped. She put the tray down, knowing what was coming next. Maggie righted her shoulders and held her head up high. This was not going to get her down. Nope.

As she looked back at the tray she'd placed on the table, she saw the glass.

Fuck it!

A smile spread across her face. She was getting kicked off the set anyway, might as well make it worth her while.

She walked back to Trevor who was standing next to Matt glaring at her. His lips were thin with anger, his jaw tense, but strangely enough, his eyes held something else.

Something she wasn't quite sure of. But she didn't care. This was her chance to stand up for herself. She took a calming breath before she honed in on Trevor. "You're a piece of shit, Trevor McCain. I hope you're able to find a way to sleep at night when you realize just how ugly you really are." Without a second thought, Maggie threw the drink in his face. She then dropped the glass on the ground and calmly walked toward the exit.

No takebacks now, Universe. You threw down the gauntlet and I picked it up and made it my bitch.

"Maggie, wait!" Danny hollered, running after her.

Nope. She didn't want to hear it. However, the moment the stage door closed behind her, Danny was there.

"Maggie, hold on, please," he begged.

"Why?" she asked, turning to face him. "I'm already being escorted off the set. Why in the world do you want me to wait?"

"Just stop walking for a second, okay?" He grabbed her hand. "Don't leave. We can work this out. Just hold on a second. I'm sorry."

Maggie looked at him like he'd lost his mind. Obviously, he was not in the same room as she was five minutes ago. "What are *you* sorry about?"

"It's just..." He looked at her. "I'm sorry that all happened."

"Don't worry about it." She shrugged. "There'll be other roles."

"It's still yours," he pleaded. "Just give us a few minutes to get everything sorted out. I wasn't lying when I said you were talented. We both saw it, me and my dad. When you're in the business you get an eye for these things. You've got the potential to make it big, Mags, just give me a second to get this all straightened out."

Mags. She felt pain in her heart. The only one who ever called her Mags was her grandmother.

Maggie looked at the security officer and then back at Danny. "If you still want me here why is he escorting me out?"

"He's not," Danny replied. "Whenever there is a problem on set, security is here to defuse it."

"It's true, Ma'am," the officer said. "Name's Rick. I just wanted to get you off the soundstage before anything else happened. Those insurance reports are a bitch to write up."

"Just give me a few minutes."

"Why are you being so nice to me?" she asked. "I just threw a drink in the face of the star of this film." *Really, what in the world was going on today? Was she in some weird Twilight Zone?*

"'Cause he deserved it," Rick mumbled.

"He's right." Danny winked at her. "The only thing that would've been better, is if you'd decked him."

"Then there would have definitely been an incident to

write on the report," Rick grumbled. "It would have been awesome to see, but I really don't fancy doing any of the work that goes with it."

Maggie tried not to laugh. Despite the situation she found herself in, it did feel good to let all of that out. She turned back to Danny. "I get he's a dick and deserved it, but why are you being so nice to me? It's not like *I'm* the star or anything."

Danny smiled at her. "Like I told you, I can see your talent. I like you. I was hoping maybe..." He shrugged. "Maybe we could be friends?"

It was as if the gravity of the situation was wiped away. *Friends.*

"Yeah." Maggie's face lit. "I'd like that."

"Great!" A wide smile spread across Danny's face. "Rick, take her to the green room. Relax there for a little bit, Mags. I'll get everything worked out and come get you so we can finish your scene."

Maggie couldn't help the happiness she felt as she watched Danny run back into the building.

"Come on, Maggie," Rick remarked. "Is it all right if I call you Maggie?"

"Yes, of course it is." Maggie nodded as she looked over her shoulder one more time to see Danny entering the building.

Friends.

Chapter Three

WHAT THE FUCK JUST HAPPENED?

Trevor remained frozen like someone had slapped him across the face.

He could hear Matt talking, but he couldn't figure out what he was saying.

His blood boiled. That... that *bitch* had just thrown a drink in his face and verbally assaulted him.

Who the fuck does she think she is?

But more importantly, why in the hell had his dick taken notice?

As he felt his lower half spring to life, his eyes widened. Holy shit, what was wrong with him? Had he recently caught something?

Trevor's dick twitched again as he replayed the words in his head the frumpy bitch had spouted.

Oh God, he needed to go to the hospital. Maybe Cassie really did give him something? That's clearly the only explanation for his dick losing its ever-loving mind right now.

"Trevor?"

"What?" An intern was standing next to him with a towel

in her hand. He snatched it from her, wiping the drink off his face.

What in the hell was going on right now? Trevor couldn't control his reactions no matter how hard he tried. Had he walk into an alternate Universe? Because that's what it seemed like.

"Trevor, are you okay?" Matt asked.

"Yeah," he mumbled into the towel. "Please tell me she's being escorted off the lot?" Once he was dry, he threw the towel at the intern before turning his head to look at the soundstage door making sure she was actually gone.

Matt looked at the crew. "Take five!"

As everyone started to leave, Trevor saw Matt gesture to an office nearby. He followed, but not before he once again looked over his shoulder at the stage door to see if the chubby girl had actually left.

As soon as he realized what he was doing, he stopped with a shake of his head.

What was wrong with him? And why was his dick still fighting against the front of his pants? Every time he thought of... he didn't know her name, he could swear he'd grown a few more impossible inches.

Trevor glared down at the front of his pants, his eyes narrowing. "Betraying bastard."

Unfortunately, he must have been just loud enough for Matt to hear because he looked back at him, his eyebrow cocked in question. "What?" Matt asked, perplexed.

"Nothing," Trevor grumbled. "Can you please explain to me why that lunatic was on set in the first place?"

"She's perfect for the part," Danny answered, appearing in the doorway.

Trevor stood with his back to the window as Matt sat down at the desk. "And what makes you a good judge of that?" Trevor mocked. "Aren't you only here because your daddy said it was okay to come to work today?" He looked at Matt. "Take your kid to work day, right?" He knew it was a low blow, he and Matt had been friends for a while, but Trevor didn't care. Right now, he was pissed and wanted answers.

"I really wish she would have decked you." Danny glared at him, his lips in a thin line with disdain.

Trevor shot his head to Danny, his fist clenching at this side. If Danny wanted someone to get hit, he'd gladly oblige to that. He was ready to teach him a lesson, when Matt spoke. "Okay, both of you, enough." Matt shook his head slightly as he stood only to perch himself on top of the desk. "Let's see if we can't all come to some sort of compromise."

"A compromise?" Trevor asked, giving him a look of pure insanity. "Are you shittin' me right now? Screw this." He reached into his pocket to pull out his phone. "I'm calling my agent."

"Trevor, you know you don't want to do that. This movie is slated to be the movie of the summer. The role was practically written for you," Matt reminded him.

Trevor hated that. No matter what was going on, Matt was always the voice of reason. *Fucking asshole.*

"Then if it was written for me, can you explain why *I*, the main character, was just physically assaulted out there?" He jerked his thumb behind him pointing toward the soundstage.

"You can't deny you didn't deserve it," Danny remarked.

"Are you kidding me?" Trevor moved to where Danny stood. He had a good few inches on the kid. He could easily take him.

"I'm not." Danny looked at his dad. "It's true. You and I both know it." He looked back at Trevor, not even a little bit intimidated by him. "You're an ass, everyone knows it. Maggie was the only one with the balls enough to say it."

Maggie—that's her name? Wait, I don't give a fuck what her name is.

Trevor narrowed his eyes dangerously at Danny. When did people start fighting against the star in the film? *He* was the reason the film would be a success. His demands *needed* to be met.

End of story.

Except...

There was something inside of him that liked the push-back Maggie had given him. Hell, it even put a fire in this brownnoser's ass.

Trevor shook his head trying to dismiss his thoughts. Why the fuck did he even care?

Then it occurred to him. "Oh, man. Now, I get it. It makes perfect sense why she's even here." He looked Danny up and down. "You're fucking her, aren't you?" Trevor shrugged smugly. "Fat girls need love too, I guess."

Danny physically paled before his face morphed into anger.

Trevor had to hold back his smirk. Despite all that was happening, this was probably one of the best days he'd had in a long time.

Finally. Finally, someone was standing up to him. He missed getting into arguments and scuffles. He missed the adrenaline rush they caused.

Something was wrong, though. If Danny really was sleeping with her, that meant she probably wouldn't sleep with him—

Trevor blanched. *Abort! Abort! Do not go down that path. What the fuck! She's not even your type. Never in your life have you liked someone that had...* as his mind went to say excess fat, but it instantly changed it to, curves. *Curves? When in the hell have I ever called what she had curves?*

Oh fuck, this was not good. Nope! Let Danny fuck her. He didn't give a shit. He didn't care if she was pushed up against the wall, his fist wrapped in her hair as she looked at him from over her shoulder. Her eyes showing so much fire that he could feel it deep in his core. She'd grab onto his waist pulling him closer to her body. She'd be begging, "Trevor, deeper!"

Fuck me!

Great, now his goddamn brain had taken a trip to crazy town. First his dick and now his brain.

What else was next?

Betraying fucking bastards! His body was now the enemy.

"I'm not sleeping with her!" Danny growled.

Instantly a wave of relief washed over Trevor.

Wait, what? No! Goddamn it. He didn't give a shit if Danny was sleeping with her.

She fucking assaulted him.

"I want her off the set *and* off the movie. If your son can't keep it in his pants that's not my problem." Trevor snapped his attention to Matt. "Because of *his* actions, not only did that bitch spy on me, she talked shit, untrue shit, and threw a drink in my face."

"You fuckin' deserved it." Danny stared him down. "Look at what you said about her in front of everyone. Plus, it's not like she lied." He smirked.

That's it. I'm going to punch this asshole.

"Boys." Matt stood. "I know this is not how we wanted today to go." He turned to Trevor. "We honestly have to have this scene. It's the pivotal point to how *your* character finds the map. If we took it out, we'd have to rewrite the script. Plus, we already have a shit ton of takes, all we need now is the over-the-shoulder frame. Normally, you know I would abide by your wishes no matter how asinine they are, but this time it would cost us more to recast and refilm."

"I don't care if recasting her blows the fucking budget!"

"What's your problem, man?" Danny asked. "It's only one more shot."

"She must be fucking killer in the sack if you are both sticking up for her."

"That's enough," Matt growled. "You know damn well no one is sleeping with anyone. You're just angry that someone actually took a shot at you."

Trevor narrowed his eyes at Matt, his jaw going tight. He'd love nothing more than to punch him right in the face. Unfortunately, Matt was one of the top directors in Hollywood, not to mention, they'd been friends for years.

"You know I wouldn't steer you wrong, Trevor. I really do think she's the best for the part. She's talented, and has great potential." Matt crossed his arms over his chest.

Trevor rolled his eyes. Whatever. He was over this.

"I can get this take done, and she'll be out of your hair," Matt reiterated.

Trevor looked at him, and then at Danny before he let out a deep sigh. "Fine. I'm staying on set, though, and if she does anything else, I'm gone. You got it?" He pointed to his chest.

Matt rolled his eyes before clasping his hand on Trevor's shoulder. "You got it, buddy. Whatever you say." Trevor could tell Matt wasn't taking him seriously, if the little laugh he heard had anything to do with it. *Fucking asshole.*

"I'll go get her," Danny announced before running out of the room.

Trevor stood in the office with his arms crossed over his chest. A frown formed on his face as he watched out of the window as Matt walked back onto the set.

What in the world was going on today?

The moment Maggie walked back on set with Danny at her side and the security guard right behind them Trevor felt it happen again.

Instantly, he looked down at the bulge at the front of his pants that had become even more prominent.

"For fuck's sake!"

"Cut!"

Maggie beamed as she put the empty glass down. She was beyond grateful she was able to film the scene. Although, she wasn't a fan of Trevor standing in the corner scowling at her the whole time.

If looks could kill, she'd been dead an hour ago. Whatever, nothing was going to ruin this for her.

She rolled her eyes. Maggie didn't get why he needed to be there. It's not like this shot had anything to do with his actual character in it.

No, he just wanted to stand there trying to intimidate her. Well, he could try all he wanted, she wasn't going to take his crap anymore. Let him stand there and pout like a big baby.

Maggie bit back her laugh.

Trevor was probably just pissed off she got the upper hand. Not only did she throw a drink in his face, she told everyone on set he had a small weenie. *Score one for you, Mags.*

Instantly, the image of him popped into her head causing her cheeks to heat. It actually hadn't been very small, well not from what little she could see of him. She'd made sure to keep her eyes above the waistline.

Something she now regretted.

Yeah, he might have been a complete jerk, but hey, she could still admire his body. There were no rules against that, right?

It didn't matter, though. Trevor McCain was an asshole. No longer was he going to be her fantasy guy.

Hell freaking no!

She'd rather gouge out her eyes with a rusty spoon than travel down that path again.

Nope. Trevor McCain had solidified himself in the douchebag hall of fame.

"Great job, Mags!" Danny hollered, as he jogged over to her. "How's it feel to be done with your first Hollywood movie?"

Maggie's whole face lit. What was it about Danny that just made her feel at ease? "It feels pretty damn good," she admitted. Placing her hand on his forearm, she continued, "Thanks for sticking up for me."

"Don't mention it." Danny sent her an ear to ear grin. "I'd do it for anyone who'd put Trevor in his place."

"Scene's done."

Before she could do anything, Maggie noticed a shadow tower over her. The moment she turned she was greeted with Trevor scowling at them. Well, not at them... but more at her hand on Danny's arm.

"She needs to leave now," Trevor snapped.

"You're such an ass." Danny jerked his head toward the door. "Come on, Mags. Let's get your stuff. I can walk you back to your car."

Maggie rolled her eyes as she ignored Trevor. She would have loved to argue with Trevor, but honestly, she just wanted to be away from him.

"Thanks, D!" Maggie replied happily, with a little more joy than was needed. Might as well showboat the fact she won while she still had the chance. "Just so you know, you're pretty amazing, Danny. Thanks for all you did for me. I had a blast."

"I wasn't lying when I said I thought you were good. You had fun 'cause it was easy for you. Come on, let's get your bag."

As she made her way out, Maggie looked over her shoulder as she walked to the stage door. "Thanks again, Matt!" The fact Maggie could see Trevor in her peripheral vision still scowling made her smile ten times wider.

Suck it, dickwad!

Maggie followed behind Danny as they got her things. As

they were making their way down the hall, Danny stopped. He touched his earpiece, holding up his hand for her to wait. After a few seconds, he spoke. "All right, I'll be right there."

Danny looked at her with a sad expression. "Maggie, I'm sorry, but they need me back on set." He pointed toward the door at the end of the hall. "If you head down that way, your car will be right outside."

"Thanks, Danny. Really, for everything you did today, thank you."

"No worries. You did a great job." He turned her in the right direction. "I'll see you soon, okay?"

"Sure," she said, hoping it was true.

"I've got your number from the casting. I'll text you when I'm done here today. Maybe we can hang out?"

"I'd like that," she agreed.

Danny suddenly had a strange look on his face. Then she realized they were talking to him in the earpiece again. "I really gotta go. I'll talk to you soon, just go straight down that hall." He then took off in a jog.

Maggie watched as Danny disappeared before she made her way toward the door. She was still a little overwhelmed, but she was happy. It'd been an extremely eventful day. Although it had started out horribly wrong in every way she could imagine, in the end, she came out on top.

That's right, Universe! You take that and suck it!

She grinned as she walked down the hall. Things were finally looking up.

Then out of nowhere, something blocked her exit.

Maggie instinctively took a step back. After balancing herself, she looked up only to be met by the glare of the one person she hoped never to see again.

"Maggie."

/ Chapter Four

TREVOR LOOKED down the hall from the room he was in to see Maggie coming his way.

His eyes instantly narrowed on her. Not only did she screw up his fuck session, but she'd somehow made his body turn against him, too.

Which was more and more evident as she made her way closer to him. For some fucking reason, his prick hadn't gotten the message that he wasn't attracted to someone of her.... physique.

Trevor purposely planned it so that when she passed the door, he jumped into the hallway. He wasn't the least bit surprised she almost collided right into him.

What a shame. That would've been perfect. Her round body rubbing against his as she tried to steady herself. He bit back a moan. *Wait a second. What the hell? Stop it for fuck's sake!*

"Maggie," he sneered, angrier at himself for his screwed-up thoughts.

Maggie's eyes widened in shock for a brief moment before she recovered. Once she realized it was him, she crossed her arms over her chest and popped her hip to one side ready for a fight.

Good.

"What's your deal?" she scoffed, shifting her balance to her other foot.

Trevor glared at her. What was *her* damn deal? *She* was the one who screwed up his day, not the other way around. She should be thanking him for not pressing charges.

Now that gave him an idea...

"What's my deal?" he asked, mirroring her stance. He made sure to flex his muscles. Intimidation was key in these types of situations. The sooner she left, the sooner he could get his body back to its normal behavior.

"Yeah, smartass, that's what I asked. Or are you really as dumb as you look? Here let me go slower for you. Whhhaatt iiss youuur ddeeaalll? That slow enough for you to comprehend there, jackass?"

He was going to strangle her. "I'll tell you my deal. You need to watch where you're going. You nearly ran me over just now. You could cause serious damage with those hips and thighs."

"Screw you, asshole. You jumped out in front of me."

"And, you need to thank me. I could have gotten you arrested for that little stunt you pulled back there." He smirked looking down at her shocked expression. He liked the fact his words seemed to take her off guard, if only for a split second.

Maggie threw her hands in the air, almost making him take a step back. "You've got to be kidding me. Dude, you really are a piece of work, you know that? I'm surprised anyone still wants to work with you at all in this business. And let's not get me started on the fact that you still have women falling all over you with that attitude. If you were my man, I'd have knocked the shit out of you a long ass time ago." With that, Maggie pushed past him, her hips brushing his as she walked by.

Instantly Trevor felt his dick twitch. *Jesus fucking Christ!* Something was seriously wrong with his junk. Ignoring his stupid body, he chased after her. "Trust me, you'd never get a man like me."

"Ha," Maggie huffed as he caught up to her. "Like I'd ever want a man like you. No thanks. I have enough going on. I don't have time to deal with someone that cries like a baby when he didn't get his way. *Screw* that!"

"I don't cry—"

"You know," Maggie interrupted him. "You're just pissed because I won." She stopped walking and turned to face him. "That's right, Trevor McCain, I won. You didn't get to have your way this time." She smirked. "And, I insulted your pecker in front of everyone."

"Bullshit, Maggie," he snarled, moving to get closer to her trying to intimidate her, but the look on her face showed he was failing. "The only reason you think you won is because your little boyfriend begged his dad."

Maggie rolled her eyes, which only caused his lower half to jump once more. Why is it that his body loved her little spout of defiance?

"Do you really have nothing better to do than to harass me?" she asked, crossing her arms over her chest. To his utter carnage, his eyes darted directly to her breasts.

"I'm not harassing you, sweetheart," he spat, once he pulled his eyes away. "I also don't see you denying the fact he's your boyfriend. What, you fuck him to get this part?"

"What's your problem, really? You must have no friends and no life if you need to be out here harassing me as I walk to my car *to leave*. You have got some serious issues, dude."

"I have friends!" Trevor cringed the second the words flew

out of his mouth. It'd come out with such desperation he *knew* she was going to mock him.

Yeah, he did have friends... not friends he could trust. They would come to hang out at this house all the time. Drink his booze, eat his food, and then leave. But fuck her, they were still his friends.

To his surprise, instead of doing what he thought she was going to do, Maggie cocked her head slightly to the side, her face washing with a hint of pity as she looked at him.

Something inside of him flipped. He didn't need her pity.

"I'm glad to hear that," she said a little more softly. Her words still dripped with disdain but they were no longer venomous.

Oh shit! Backtrack, backtrack!

Not only had Maggie put him in his place, she nearly had him all figured out within a matter of minutes. And damned if his dick didn't like that too.

He really needed to see a doctor before the thing actually fell off.

"Make sure you knock before you open doors next time. With your luck, you'll piss off someone else and be exiled from Hollywood." With those parting words, Trevor turned on his heel and walked back into the building.

WHAT THE HELL WAS THAT?

Maggie started her car, still trying to understand what the heck had just happened. It was almost as if his last words were meant to be mean but instead turned out to be a weird friendly warning.

Nahhhh.

Maggie shook her head. Trevor was just being a dick. Nothing new there. She sighed. It sucked her image of him was now tarnished. This is why she was so hesitant about meeting her heroes in person.

Now, she was going to have to rearrange her fantasies.

The second she got home she was burning all of her movies and memorabilia of him. *Burn, baby, burn!*

It didn't matter how attractive Trevor was. How his muscles rippled when he crossed his arms over his chest, or how his gaze could somehow look deep inside of her... Almost as if he was looking into her soul.

Nope.

He was a dickhead. A huge dickhead. Not only did he make fun of her looks—just like everyone else in her life, except Grammie. But he did it in front of the whole freaking crew.

Maggie smirked as she turned the corner. She was glad she threw that drink in his face.

He deserved it.

As she started to laugh at his shocked expression, she snorted. He was so mad when Matt insisted she stayed to finish out her scene.

Trevor looked like such a baby as he stood in the corner glaring at her the whole time.

"Well, guess what, Trevor?" Maggie did a little dance in her car. "You could've glared until the cows came home. I still got to finish out my part and there was nothing you could do about it. How do you like them apples!"

She looked up at the roof of her car, a triumphant smile on her face. "Universe, I gave you a lot of shit this morning, but honestly, today was one of the best days of my life. I mean, that's if you take out the whole name-calling, getting lost, walking in on Trevor screwing some skank." She paused. "Actually, we're gonna say it's up there in at least my top five. Yeah, top five is good."

Maggie started to hum and tap her fingers on the steering

wheel as she continued on her drive home. No matter what, today was a good day. And if you ask her, she'd say she was the best damn waitress Hollywood had ever seen.

This was her dream in the making. She finally had a chance to be on a real film set. She acted her butt off and was rewarded. Not only did Danny, but Matt stood up for her, too. *Score two points for me!*

It was like that little pat on the back saying you didn't waste your whole life following a dead dream, as her mother called it.

"Dead dream my ass. Take that, Mommy dearest!"

Once she was home, Maggie quickly pulled into her parking spot and made her way up to her apartment.

Her mother had always hated her dream of being an actor. She made it a point every chance she got to mention how Maggie was too fat and too plain. How she needed to find a real job and a real career.

Sure, in the beginning, her mother tolerated her aspirations of being an actor. That was until she found out Grammie left all her money to Maggie so she could move to LA and follow her dream.

Okay, well that had put a damper on their relationship. A huge damper.

Maggie opened her apartment door and threw her backpack onto the beat-up couch she'd purchased at a thrift shop the first week she moved in.

"Pocket! Mommy's home."

Just then a little white and tan Siamese cat came running out to greet her. Meowing, or screaming—as Maggie liked to say, with excitement.

Maggie could swear the cat actually talked to her. She'd read online Siamese cats were vocal. She hadn't quite understood *how* vocal until she actually had one, though.

She'd named him Pocket after she found him in the pocket

of an old coat that was beside the dumpster at her apartment. She thought it was cute and he seemed to like it.

However, after a few nights, Maggie understood exactly what the internet meant when it said Siamese cats were vocal. Pocket started screaming at the top of his lungs to "let her know he was there". Half the time he sounded just like an air raid horn signaling for everyone to take cover.

Maggie plopped down onto her couch with Pocket jumping into her lap. "Did you miss your mommy?" Maggie scratched his chin. "I know you missed your mommy."

Pocket answered with a meow before curling into her lap purring.

Maggie sat there petting Pocket as she tried to make sense of the day. It had been a complete clusterfuck. And then when she finally thought she was through and could move on? Nope. Trevor showed back up.

She couldn't understand why he'd followed her out to her car, or why he was such a jerk.

Seriously, there was no need for him to continue his tirade. It was clear she was leaving.

Stupid man.

As she replayed the events she kept stopping at his reaction to the "friends'" comment.

"You know, kitty, don't get me wrong here, Trevor was still a complete asshat, but it must be hard to make real friends once you've made it big in Hollywood."

Pocket opened one piercing blue eye at her and then slowly closed it.

Man, that's creepy.

"Anyway, just think, Pocket, how do you know who your real friends are? How can you be sure they aren't there to use you, make you spend money on them, or even try to get famous through you?" The cat started to purr louder as he kneaded her thigh. "You're right. It doesn't matter. Trevor was still a jerk. Saying I couldn't get a man like him. Asshole. Like I'd ever want someone like him in the first place."

Maggie looked from Pocket to see the poster of Trevor's last movie on her wall. "Okay, so maybe at one point I would have done anything to have a man like Trevor notice me."

The cat once again opened its eye at her, judgingly.

"Okay, okay, up until twelve hours ago I wanted a man like him. Well, actually I wanted him, but that's beside the point. That ship has sailed. No more Trevor McCain in my life, Pocket. It's just you and me."

Maggie pushed Pocket off her lap and headed toward the bathroom. She needed to shower off everything that happened to her today.

Right before she made it to her bathroom, she looked over her shoulder at the poster on her wall once again. She couldn't help the feeling of pity that washed over her as she looked at Trevor's face.

Chapter Five

THAT NIGHT MAGGIE laid on her bed with Pocket curled at her side. After her shower, she'd removed the poster from her living room and gathered all her movies that had Trevor in them, and tossed them in a box in the corner.

Sure, she still respected his acting technique, but his real-life personality was something she couldn't look past. So, in the trash everything went.

Maggie's phone buzzed on her nightstand distracting her from her thoughts.

However, when she moved to retrieve it, her asshole of a cat decided that her hands were now the enemy and needed to be attacked. She tried to reach for her phone one more time as she pushed him away but Pocket declared he needed to exorcize the demon from her instead.

"Pocket, knock it off! Don't make me take you back to the dumpster."

Pocket meowed loudly at her.

With a roll of her eyes, she grabbed the phone. That's when she saw she had two text messages.

Hi Maggie, it's Danny. It was great working with you today. I hope you made it home all right?

A smile spread across her face. No matter the craziness of the day she was glad she met Danny. He was a great guy and she could absolutely see herself forming a friendship with him.

I was wondering if you'd like to get coffee tomorrow?

Just as Maggie started to reply, she was attacked by her cat, who now seemed to decide her hands were no longer the enemy, but her whole body was instead. "Do you want me to lock you out tonight, Pocket? Because I will," she threatened.

As if he was responding to her, Pocket started to bellow. Oh, how she loved the air-horn sound that came from Pocket late at night.

"If you don't knock it off, I'm not giving you the tuna that I picked up at the store yesterday."

Instantly, Pocket stop attacking her and sat like the picture-perfect animal at the end of the bed. He slowly blinked looking at her with his ice-blue eyes, as if to say, "Are you going to get me the tuna or what?"

"You're a piece of work you know that, right?" Maggie moved down the bed to scratch Pocket behind the ears. "But I wouldn't have it any other way."

She picked up her phone that had ended up in the covers during the ambush and opened the text messages from Danny.

Thank you again, even with everything that happened. I had a blast on set. Sure, I would really like to go get coffee. I haven't made any friends since moving here and it'll be nice to actually get out.

She looked back at Pocket. "If I were you, I'd start acting nicer. I could easily replace you with Danny." She pointed to her phone.

Pocket looked at her for about three seconds as he contemplated his actions. Too bad for her he decided on *attack*.

"Oh, for fuck's sake!"

TREVOR FINALLY ENDED up at home around three in the morning. After he was released from the set, he had too much energy going through him to go home.

Instead, he ended up at one of Hollywood's exclusive clubs where he knew the liquor flowed and the chicks were easy.

He needed this to clear his mind. He had no idea what was wrong with him, but he hoped after drinking enough and possibly finding some willing partners, his dick would finally be fixed. Much to his dismay, though, whenever a hot little thing started to grind on him, images of Maggie throwing the drink in his face clouded his mind.

"Fuck man!" he growled as he threw his jacket onto the couch. Not only did she ruin his day on set, but she also ruined his night.

It was like she planted some extraterrestrial mind-warping shit in his brain. Not only was his dick infected with whatever she gave him, but his mind seemed to be infected as well. "Fuck this shit." He climbed the stairs to his bedroom. Things were bound to be back to normal when he woke up.

The next morning around ten, he woke. Looking around his bedroom, he groaned. He could already tell today was going to be a shitty day.

At least he didn't have to be on set.

He crawled out of bed and slowly stripped off last night's clothes as he made his way to the bathroom. He had shit he needed to do today and didn't have time to screw around. He already slept in way later than he wanted.

He turned on the shower and hopped in. Thankfully, the feel of the hot water and steam surrounding him worked out his aching muscles, relaxing him.

He preferred drinking at home with his friends rather than going out. Somehow, whenever he ended up at the club, the next morning was always ten times worse than when he got drunk at his own place.

Trevor closed his eyes as he let the water rush over his body. Blindly, he reached for the body wash. Squirting some into his hands he lathered them and slowly started to wash away everything from yesterday and last night.

As his fingertips worked their way down his chest, images of Maggie started to pop into his mind. This time, however, instead of her throwing the drink at him, she was on her knees looking up at him. Her deep blue eyes overflowed with passion.

A groan escaped his lips.

He pictured her pink little tongue sticking out to lick her upper lip.

"Fuck," he moaned as his fingers reached the base of his already hard member. "I'll give you something to fill that mouth with," he mumbled as he started to pump himself.

"Yes baby, take it deeper, I know you can."

Images of his dick surrounded by her lips, his member

disappearing deep into her mouth sent shivers down his body. "Try to say some smart-aleck comment now, baby. Try to say it's a small dick as you swallow me whole."

His fantasy Maggie started to hum as he pumped himself harder and faster.

"Holy shit." He couldn't hold back. The image of her looking up at him was too much. He held his eyes shut as he imagined shooting his load down her throat.

Once he was sure fantasy Maggie had swallowed every drop, he rested his head on the back tile of the shower and tried to control his erratic breathing.

Out of nowhere, the realization hit him. "What the fuck did I just do?" He stumbled as he stood upright. "What in the hell is wrong with me?"

He quickly rinsed off the rest of his body and got out of the shower. Going over to the closet he grabbed a pair of sweatpants and a hoodie.

"Run. I need to go for a run."

Running always helped clear his mind. And that was exactly what he needed. He looked down at his body in disgust. "Betraying fuckin' bastard!"

Trevor made his way to his favorite spot to run within ten minutes. Normally, he'd run in his in-home gym, but on days when his mind was particularly scattered, he'd go to the park near his house.

It was a quiet area. Most people that lived around here were celebrities or wealthy and wanted to be left alone. There was a small diner, along with a hole-in-the-wall coffee shop that served the best coffee in all of California.

After running through the park, he always made sure to stop at Perk You Up on his way back. It would be his little treat for completing a good run and getting his shit back in order.

He stretched his legs, pulled his headphones out and made

sure his phone was set to his favorite running playlist, and took off.

⸻

"THIS PLACE IS ADORABLE." Maggie looked around the coffee shop. Behind the counter was a sign that said, Perk You Up. She loved the name, and she couldn't help but admire everything surrounding her. The place had huge armchairs and a comfy sofa. The walls were a deep red with artistic paintings everywhere. It couldn't help but feel homey.

"Glad you like it," Danny remarked, as he made his way to the counter. "It's a really quiet place. They never get paparazzi here."

"Why would you see them here?" she asked, looking around confused. Did Danny have paparazzi following him? And if so, why? Sure his dad was famous but—

"It's because of the neighborhood." He shrugged. "Most of the people that live around here are pretty famous."

"Okay?" She cocked her head to the side. "What does the neighborhood have anything to do with that?"

"This is pretty much a private neighborhood. No one comes in here unless invited," Danny remarked, as if it were common knowledge.

Maggie looked down at herself. How was she here then? If this was a hot place for celebrities, why did they let her in?

"Basically," Danny continued. "If someone comes in here or is walking around that doesn't look like they belong the cops are called instantly."

Oh shit! Are they coming for me?

Danny laughed. "Don't look like that. You're fine, plus..." He smiled. "You're with me."

"So, who are these people that report strange individuals walking around?"

"Everyone does. Everyone looks out for each other. The shops here including Perk You Up have been here forever. It's kind of like our private community and we look out for one another."

"Makes sense, I guess." She walked up to the counter.

The barista looked at her and then at Danny. Smiling warmly, her whole face lit. "Danny, it's so nice to see you! It's been a few weeks."

"Hey, Lexi."

Maggie watched as Danny's eyes brightened. She then looked back at the barista. She was cute, around her age maybe a little younger. She wore her hair in two buns on top of her head that were highlighted with purple and blue. She had a great smile that showed pearly white teeth behind deep red lips. She had that classic pin-up look—a little curvy but in all the right places.

Not like her.

Nope. Maggie's extra curves just poured out of her and made her lumpy and bumpy. No, this Lexi chick knew how to rock her curves. She had a style all her own. The confidence just radiated off her. She could tell right off the bat when Lexi walked into a room she owned the place.

Maggie couldn't help but wonder why she was working as a barista at a coffee shop, though. Her energy and personality seemed to be so much bigger than that.

"I've been on set a lot the past couple weeks," Danny continued. "We've been getting there so early in the morning you aren't even open yet."

"Such a shame," Lexi remarked. "I don't like not getting my daily dose of Danny." Lexi winked at him causing Danny's face to heat.

This chick is good!

"I'll make your drink," Lexi announced, already turning around to start the order. Once she had the espresso machine started, she turned back to Maggie. "And what can I get you, sweet thing?"

Maggie beamed. There was something about Lexi that was intoxicating. "I'll have a soy caramel macchiato with an extra shot of espresso, please."

Lexi cocked her head to the side. "Is that normally what you like to drink?" she asked.

Maggie nodded a little confused.

Lexi looked her up and down. "I'm going to make you something a little different to try." Lexi smiled so wide her teeth showed. "Let's just say this is my special magic power."

Maggie turned toward Danny who was agreeing. "It's true. She knows what's good for you only after speaking to you for a few minutes."

"All right." Maggie's brows pulled together. "I'll try anything once."

"Good to know." Danny threw back his head and laughed.

"You two go find a spot to sit down. I'll bring over your drinks in a moment."

With that, Danny and Maggie made their way over to the corner of the room where two mismatched armchairs were. She really did like this place and hoped to be able to come back here with or without Danny.

After a few moments of settling in, Lexi brought over their two drinks along with two biscottis.

"Hope you don't mind," Lexi said. "I know Danny really likes them, so I brought you a biscotti as well."

"I love them," Maggie said as she reached for her drink.

Lexi stood there clearly waiting for her to take the first sip.

Understanding what she wanted Maggie watched Lexi over the rim of the mug as she took the first sip. As soon as the liquid hit her tongue she was thrown into a wave of euphoria. "Holy freaking hell! What is this? It's like heaven in my mouth!" Maggie took another sip ignoring the gleeful shout and happy dance that came from Lexi.

"I told you she was good," Danny remarked while drinking his own concoction.

"It's what I do best." Lexi's smile went from ear to ear. "The biscotti is homemade. Let me know what you think of them. I'll be behind the counter if either of you need anything." She winked at Danny.

"I'm pretty sure I'm in love with you," Maggie moaned as Lexi turned to leave while she took another sip of her drink.

Without missing a beat, Lexi looked over her shoulder. "Back at cha, puddin' pop."

"No for real, you have just become my best friend!" Maggie's eyes rolled to the back of her head as she took yet another sip.

"I'm always down for more best friends," Lexi remarked, as she walked away. When she made it to the counter she looked back and hollered, "If you need anything, let me know."

"Sure thing, Lex," Danny said before turning back to Maggie.

Maggie got comfortable on the chair as Danny put his drink down and reached for the treat.

"So, Maggie, I wanted to talk to you about what happened yesterday."

Oh no!

THE RUN WAS EXACTLY what Trevor needed. He finally felt like his mind was clear. Plus, it also helped he was just rounding the corner to his favorite coffee shop. It was by far the best coffee in all of California. And Lexi, the girl behind the counter, knew exactly what he needed the second she saw him without even asking. He hoped he'd get something with a couple extra shots today along with one of her delicious home-made treats. Damn, that girl knew how to bake.

Trevor was already excited for whatever concoction Lexi was going to come up with. There was something about her he just loved. Well, he wasn't attracted to her, but why would he be? Plus, she reminded him of Maggie now.

Maggie.

Great. Now he was annoyed again. Somewhere along his run, he had forgotten about her, and now...wham she was back to the front of his mind.

He shook his head trying to dislodge Maggie from his thoughts as he walked up to the counter grinning at Lexi.

Trevor surveyed the room briefly only to pull back and look at Lexi as she was turned around making his drink.

I'm fucking losing it, he thought as he made sure to keep his focus on what Lexi was doing. He could swear when he looked around the coffee shop he saw Maggie sitting in the corner.

This was not good.

This was not good at all. What the hell was he going to do? He'd honestly lost his mind. There was no way Maggie was there.

Trevor pinched his eyes roughly together as he rubbed his forehead.

He knew what he needed to do.

He needed to get laid. Once he did, his body would go back to normal and his mind would stop playing tricks on him.

Just in case, though, carefully, he looked out of the corner of his eye.

Shit!

Nope, Maggie was there. This wasn't a vision. This was fucking real.

He then peered over the rack of coffee cups to see who she was talking to.

You gotta be fucking kidding me!

All thoughts of his drink disappeared as he stormed over to them. "And you say you're not fucking?" he sneered.

"Ahhh! Don't do that." Maggie's hand when to her heart before she stared up at him. "What?"

Trevor turned to Danny ignoring her. "Let me guess. Is she auditioning for her next role?"

"Excuse you?" Danny's brows shot up.

"Let me give you some free advice, Maggie." He turned back to her. "Fuck someone that's more important than him. Maybe then you'll get a bigger role, instead of some no-name extra."

As Maggie jumped from her seat he instantly saw the fury in her eyes. There was so much passion and rage staring back at him. Her eyes almost matched what he had pictured in the shower earlier that morning.

Oh fuck. No.

"Listen here, jerk! No one, and I mean no one, talks to me or my friends like that!" She narrowed her eyes dangerously at him. "Are you following me?" Maggie spat.

"Me?" He pointed to himself, laughing. "Following you? Only in your dreams, sweetheart." He inwardly cursed himself for calling her sweetheart.

"Looks like it to me," she shot back. "I've been here with Danny for a while now. *You're* the one that showed up after us. Looks like stalking to me."

"What are *you* doing in this neighborhood? That's a better question." His neighborhood was supposed to be his sanctuary. She was *never* supposed to be there.

"She's with me," Danny answered, standing up. "What's your problem, Trevor?"

"My problem is her." Trevor snapped his finger to Maggie.

"Is it that you hate all fat women, or is it just me?" Maggie crossed her arms over her chest causing his eyes to hone in directly on her ample rack.

He nearly choked when he felt his dick tighten once again.

"Trevor, why are you harassing my best friend?" Lexi walked over to the group scowling him.

"Best friend? Yeah, right." Trevor's jaw tightened. She cannot be Lexi's best friend. No way in hell would he allow that. That would mean Maggie would be here all the time. No fucking way.

Before he could say anything a deep growl came from Maggie. "What the fuck crawled up your ass? You really need to grow up."

If she wanted to fight, he was ready for it.

Her eyes narrowed on him. "The likelihood of us running into each other was pretty slim, but look at us now. You're gonna have to get over whatever your problem is, jerk face. I'm *not* leaving LA and if you have a problem with that, you can kiss my fat white Irish ass!" Maggie picked up her bag and pushed her way past him.

Without thinking, Trevor grabbed her arm. "Where do you think you're going?"

Instantly, Maggie jerked out of his grasp. Unfortunately for him though, as soon as she was free, she slapped him in the face. "Do *not* touch me. Never touch me!"

Maggie stormed toward the door but Trevor was right behind her. "Don't worry, *Maggie*. No one would ever want to touch you." He could have kicked himself in the face for his next words. "You're the one that probably wants to touch me."

Maggie turned around so fast his head almost spun.

"Trust me, *little* man. I wouldn't touch you even for a million dollars."

Danny stood next to her. "Maggie?"

"No worries, Danny." She faced the bane of his existence at the moment. "I'll text you in a bit. We'll talk about the fundraiser then."

Maggie then looked at Lexi. "You and I will definitely be seeing more of each other. I don't think I can live without this coffee now."

"That's a promise." Lexi winked.

"Shit," Danny started. "Maggie I'm sorry. I didn't mean—"

"No worries," Maggie interrupted him.

As he watched everything play out, Trevor knew he was scowling at her. But the fact she wasn't even acknowledging him pissed him off.

Look at me. Not him! The thought clouded his mind before he realized what he was doing. What the hell was wrong with him?

"We'll talk about the fundraiser later. See ya, Danny." With that, Maggie walked out of the coffee shop, leaving him just standing there.

Once he no longer could see her through the window, he turned to see Lexi scowling at him.

"I should deny you your coffee today."

Pushing Maggie out of this mind, he turned on the charm. "Now, baby, you'd never do that." He gave Lexi a toothy grin.

Lexi's brows pulled together. As she stared him down she let out a heavy sigh. "You're right about the coffee. But you get zero goodies."

Anger raced through him again. *Now Maggie cost me my goodies! Could today get any worse?*

"You know McCain, you're a real ass."

Trevor turned to see Danny picking up his stuff shaking his head.

"Whatever." Ignoring Danny, Trevor grumbled before turning back to Lexi.

Maybe I can sweet talk her into a muffin?

However, just as he was about to open his mouth, Maggie's words registered through his mind. Instantly, Trevor snapped to Danny. "What fundraiser?"

Danny shrugged.

"You don't mean the charity event the studio is putting on? Oh, hell no!"

No fucking way!

Trevor's eyes narrowed on Danny, as the dumbass smirked at him.

"Fuck no," Trevor sneered. No way in hell was he going to let Maggie in there. She'd look so out of place. She'd probably have a dress on that showed all her curves, something that would make her eyes pop with color. Her hair would be done and she'd be on the arm of *Danny.*

His fists clenched at his sides as he watched a shit-eating grin appear on Danny's face.

No. Hell no.

Over his dead body.

Chapter Six

MAGGIE ARRIVED BACK at her apartment, still fuming from her latest encounter with Trevor. Honestly, what in the hell had she done in a past life to deserve this? She tried to do right by the Universe. Tried to be a good citizen and yet, somehow, the Universe decided to shit on her every chance it got.

She scoffed before she plopped onto the couch with a heavy sigh.

Okay, so it wasn't all that bad. Danny had been extremely nice, and the coffee shop was perfect in every way possible.

Not to mention Lexi was officially now her best friend, be damned what anyone said. Lexi was a master at all things coffee and Perk You Up was now Maggie's favorite spot in all of Los Angeles.

As she settled into her seat Pocket jumped onto her lap demanding to be pet. "You know, you're a little pushy, Kitty."

Pocket bellowed as loud as he could before he dropped onto his side and swatted Maggie's arm to have her commence the petting.

"Fine." Maggie rolled her eyes as she chuckled. When she

started scratching Pocket on his belly, she was instantly rewarded with an attack, as he held on and kicked his back legs onto her arm as hard as he could.

"My arm is not a rat," Maggie gritted, as she tried to pry her arm away from the possessed creature.

Pocket stopped the attack, only for one brief moment while he looked at her with an ice-blue stare.

"Don't you look at me in that tone of voice," Maggie snapped. "You started it."

The cat let go of her hand only to sit up in her lap before pouncing on her all over again.

"Oh, for the love of all things." Maggie grabbed the cat in mid-air and placed him on the floor. "I swear, I'll never be able to bring anyone over here with the way you act!"

Pocket seemingly took offense to the remark turned his nose up at Maggie and walked out of the living room like he was the king of freakin' England into the kitchen. Maggie rolled her eyes again. She loved that cat, but sometimes...

Sighing she sat back on the couch closing her eyes. "I wonder if Lexi or Danny would be able to tolerate you long enough to have dinner or watch a movie?"

Right on cue, a meow came from the kitchen.

"You're right. No one can tolerate you."

Blocking out the cat, Maggie took a calming breath. Despite the morning's unfortunate turn of events, she did have a good time with Danny and Lexi.

Plus, Lexi was a coffee goddess. Maggie needed to learn what was in that glorious drink Lexi made for her. It was like nectar from the gods. The drink rolled over her tongue like a hot man taking off his shirt to oil himself up.

Mmmmm, good.

Too bad it was ruined with stupid Trevor.

Los Angeles was huge and had millions of people in it.

What were the chances that she'd end up at a coffee shop in *his* neighborhood?

Once again, the Universe was clearly out to get her.

Maggie huffed into the air as she closed her eyes. She needed to figure out her Universe subscription and cancel it or at least change the preferences. "Is this because I refused to call my mom? Or is it because I threw that drink in his stupid face?" She glared at the ceiling. "Probably the drink."

Maggie stood, stretching, as she made her way to the kitchen to see what her devil cat was up to. However, she was about halfway to her destination when her phone rang.

When she looked at it, she didn't recognize the number. Thinking it could be a callback she took a deep breath and answered as professionally as possible. "Maggie Connelly here."

"Maggie?" a voice came over the line.

"Yes, this is she."

"Yay!" the woman squealed. *"I'm glad you answered. This is Lexi from Perk You Up. Danny gave me your number."*

A chuckle escaped her as she relaxed into a grin. Lexi was everything Maggie wanted to be. She oozed this confidence that just drew people to her like a fish to water. Not only that, she took Trevor down a notch. And, how could she possibly forget she made the best damn coffee in all the world. First thing tomorrow morning she knew *exactly* where she was headed. "Oh hey, Lexi. How's it going?"

"I'm doing bea-u-ti-ful. I wanted to ask if you would like to hang out tonight? Maybe grab a bite to eat. Danny hinted you were somewhat new to town and—"

"Yes!" Maggie cut her off. She'd do anything Lexi wanted. Bow down at her altar if she'd demanded it. You don't mess with someone that can take one look at you and fix all your problems with one mouthwatering drink.

"That's what I like to hear," Lexi purred.

Maggie hit her forehead with the palm of her hand. *Way to act normal, Mags. Why don't you just flash a neon sign above your head saying "Desperate"?* "It's been pretty boring here in L.A. by myself. I haven't gotten out much unless it was to audition."

"Exactly my point. I close Perk You Up at 4:30 today. Do you wanna meet then?"

"Yeah. I'd really like that." She smiled as she walked into her kitchen.

"Great! See you then. We'll talk all about Trevor."

Maggie froze, but before she could say anything, Lexi hung up.

"Damn it!"

As she worried her bottom lip, Maggie looked down at Pocket. The jerk glanced up at her, slowly blinking with judgement in his eyes.

TREVOR PACED AROUND his bedroom as he berated Matt on the phone. "This is complete bullshit! There is absolutely no reason she needs to be there."

Matt sighed on the other end of the line. *"I honestly don't know what your problem is with her, Trevor. You met her once. She is really a sweet girl if you got to know her. Plus, she's got balls. Cut her some slack."*

"Cut her some slack? Are you fucking kidding me right now? She walked in on me fucking Cassandra or Cassie. I don't remember what her name was, but that doesn't matter," he spat as he continued to pace. What in the world was wrong with everyone? Normally, he'd ask for something and there would be no questions asked. God forbid he asked for the girl that threw a drink in his face to be banned from the fundraiser. It wasn't like he was asking for a virgin sacrifice or some shit like that.

"Far be it from me to point out that you should not *have been screwing anyone on set to begin with. I'm also going to overlook the fact that you don't even remember her name."*

"Matt," Trevor started. "We've known each other a long time. I'm only asking for this one thing."

"Trevor, I hate to have to bring this to your, oh so delicate ego, but you ask for shit all the time."

Trevor groaned. "And you always get me what I ask for."

"You know I'd do anything for you, you're my star. You're a damn fine actor. But, I can't do this. You know the whole cast and crew are welcome to the event. It's in everyone's contract. Might I point out, the contract that has already been signed."

In his annoyance, Trevor disconnected his phone and threw it onto a nearby chair as the anger ran through him.

This was all *her* fault. Before Maggie, no one questioned him. And now everyone was questioning him. Even freaking Lexi gave him crap.

Had this frumpy nobody gone around and cast a spell on everyone or some shit like that?

Trevor slumped onto his bed. Maybe he could call his agent and tell them he wouldn't be showing up to the fundraiser? He groaned. *Damnit.* He knew he *had* to show up. Everyone else's contract would let them be *invited* to the event. He had no choice *but* to be there.

He hated these things. They were never any fun. Everyone was always trying to one-up each other. It was the typical Hollywood bullshit. Normally he'd find a chick, get drunk with her and make a game of trying to screw in any room possible until the function was over. It was the only way he could pass the time...

I wonder if Maggie could be that woman?

Trevor shot off the bed nearly stumbling over. "What the absolute fuck?"

All right, now he knew he needed to make an appointment with the doctor.

SITTING across from Lexi at a trendy hipster café, Maggie picked at her vegan sandwich to take a bite.

Wait, could you even call it a sandwich? All the sandwiches she'd ever eaten had a huge hunk of meat in the middle, followed by a slathering of mayo or mustard, sometimes both, and maybe, just maybe, some lettuce if she was feeling particularly "healthy" for the day.

"You don't like it?" Lexi pouted before she took another bite of her food.

"No, it's good." The food wasn't bad, it was just something she wasn't used to.

"Liar!" Lexi sang as she finished her last bite. "Mmmm, this place is so good."

Maggie laughed at Lexi's antics. "I'm just not used to this type of food."

"Huh?" Lexi remarked. "I thought all you actors ate super healthy."

Maggie pointed at her curves with a chuckle. "Not me."

Lexi dropped her napkin as she stared Maggie down. "Did you just make fun of your weight? I know homegirl did not just make fun of herself in front of me."

Maggie not knowing what to do or say, just looked at her. She always made sure to make fun of her weight before someone else could. It's the only defense she had. But she'd never had someone call her out on it before.

"I've got at least a good fifteen pounds on you, if not more." Lexi stood doing a full turn as she shimmied her hips.

"Rock what you've got, girl. You and me, we've got curves for days. It's what drives the men wild."

"What men?" Maggie cocked her brow.

Universe, if you're listening, send these men my way.

"All the men, chica." Lexi smirked. "You just gotta shake what ya momma gave you and they drop to their knees."

Maggie barked out a heartfelt laugh at Lexi as she shook her head. "You and I live in two completely different worlds."

"Nope, same world. You just don't believe in yourself." Lexi looked around the café before looking back at her. "Yep same world."

Well, this just took a turn she did not want to go down. "I didn't get the memo that this was a come to Jesus meeting."

That had Lexi throwing her head back in laughter. "Maggie, I like you. You got a spunk to you that I can't get enough of. No wonder you've caught Trevor's eye."

Now it was Maggie's turn to burst into laughter. "If by caught, you mean he is trying to destroy me? Then yes, we can say I caught his eye."

"Trevor can be an asshole. Trust me, I've known him long enough to completely understand that. Trevor and jerk go hand in hand." Lexi reached over and grabbed Maggie's food bringing it to her side.

"So, then you get what I am talking about. He was a complete ass to me on set the other day and I didn't do anything to him. Okay fine, technically, I did walk in on him, but that's beside the point. It was an accident."

"Relax, relax," Lexi replied around a mouthful of food. "Danny told me all about it."

"Let's not forget about the whole scene in the coffee shop this morning."

"Total prick," Lexi agreed. "I'm on your side here. Chicks before dicks any day."

Maggie laughed. Lexi was a piece of work, but man did she

love it. *Thank you, Universe, for finally giving me something good. Between Lexi and Danny, I think I might actually make it here in a town of failed dreams.* She smiled as she sipped on her green-leaf, weird smoothie.

"I've learned Trevor is someone you have to control with a gentle hand. Not too firm or he'll know you're controlling him."

"So how in the world do you know this if the only time you see him is when he comes in for coffee?"

"Hey, coffee is an art form. In some ways, I'm like a weird bartender. I know everyone's secrets. It's always written all over their faces in the early morning. I get a good look at them before they get their first sip of coffee goodness and their mask drops into place."

"You are something else." Maggie laughed giving her a smile.

"You laugh, but it's how I know exactly what to make someone what they *need*. One look at their face and I just know. It's like a sixth sense."

Maggie cocked her head to the side. "That's kind of creepy."

"Might be creepy but it hasn't failed me yet." Lexi stood before pushing her chair in. She motioned to the door. "Come on chica, there is this kick-ass hot dog place about a five-minute walk from here."

"Oh, hell yeah!" Maggie jumped to her feet and followed Lexi out of the restaurant. Give her mystery meat any day. She'd gladly take it over whatever the hell she just had.

Lexi hooked her arm around Maggie's as they walked down the street. "Okay, now that we are out of the earshot of nosy people... Spill it, sister, how big is Trevor's ding dong?"

Fuck me.

Chapter Seven

THANKFULLY, Trevor wasn't needed on set at the butt crack of dawn the next morning, which was a rare occurrence. So, he took full advantage of it and leisurely made his way to Perk You Up. When he got there, however, he was confronted with the accusing eyes of his favorite barista.

"Hey, sweet cheeks." He winked at Lexi as he walked up to the counter. "Why the long face?"

Lexi huffed as she narrowed her eyes at him. "What makes you think I'm not still upset with you for being rude to one of my customers?"

Trevor rolled his eyes. Could he not go five minutes without being reminded of Maggie? She was everywhere. Last night after Trevor realized he wasn't getting his way with Matt, he took a shower. Maggie immediately made her appearance again and his stupid dick took notice. When he'd heated up some leftover food, he'd ended up picturing Maggie sitting across from him as she nibbled on some fruit —topless.

Something was seriously wrong with him.

His annoyance came back. He should've known better

than to come to Perk You Up. "I thought you said *best friend* yesterday?"

Lexi's face lit before she turned on her heel and started making his drink with a stupid pep in her step. "Oh, best friend for sure," she sang, which annoyed him more. "That girl is a-w-e-some. Horrible taste in food, but a hell of a lot of fun. Did you know she can impersonate someone only after meeting them for a few minutes?" She turned back handing him his drink.

"No. I didn't." His eye twitched as held the cup a little tighter.

"She can. I actually didn't know she could until we got to the hot dog place on Rosen. You know the one with the crazy eccentric cook that talks with his hands and speaks so fast you can't understand him?"

Trevor assumed she wasn't really asking him because she kept talking.

"We get our food and all of a sudden Maggie's impersonating him. She was great at it. I could swear I was watching him right in front of me. Well, you know except for the fact that he's a crazy old dude and Maggie's got a vagina. But putting that aside, it was like watching two of him."

Instantly after hearing the words Maggie and vagina, Trevor's mind went to her beneath him, in front of him, and on top of him. He had to bite the inside of his cheek to keep from moaning. *Seriously, I need to make that doctor's appointment.*

"Within minutes Maggie was doing everyone. I'd throw out a name of someone and boom! Man, her impersonations are spot freakin' on." Lexi looked him up and down before winking at him. "Should have heard her do you. I almost peed myself I laughed so hard."

Her do you...Fuck!

His body tightened. Letting out a deep breath, he placed

his coffee on the counter. "Sounds like you two got very chummy. Don't know why, though. She seems like someone that would just annoy the shit out of you."

"Nope," Lexi answered as a toothy grin appeared on her face. "That'd be you."

"You know," he responded, before reaching for his coffee. "You used to be my favorite barista. Just so you know, you've recently been demoted."

Lexi held her hand over her heart and threw herself onto the wall behind her. "However will I live?"

"You know you should have been an actor with all your dramatics." Trevor glared at her.

"Then who would be here to serve you the best damn cup of coffee you've ever had?" she asked, moving over to the baked goods retrieving a blueberry muffin, and handing it to him.

"I take it back. *You're* the most annoying person," he growled before grabbing the muffin as he turned to leave.

"You're only saying that because you know Maggie spilled all the beans. I never pictured you only packing a *small* pencil."

The coffee cup instantly dropped from his hand collapsing onto the floor before he turned around.

✦

TODAY WAS SUPPOSED to be a relaxing day for Maggie. She was going to take some much needed time to regroup. She ended up having a lot of fun last night with Lexi. It was good to get out of the apartment and actually be in civilization doing normal things for once.

Unfortunately, her plans were derailed around ten. Danny called to inform her she was needed on set at eleven. Apparently during the last part of filming something went wrong and the footage wasn't usable. Most of the scene was salvage-able, however, the end was not. Rather than just cutting it all together they wanted her to refilm.

At first, Maggie was a little hesitant. Sure, she wanted to film again. What actor wouldn't want to be on set?

That wasn't the problem, though.

She just really didn't want to run into Trevor again.

After about five minutes Danny had convinced her that she'd be done and off set before Trevor would even show up for the day. His call time apparently wasn't until four.

And after having a debate with her loud-mouth, very opinionated cat, she finally completely gave in. So, what if she did run into Trevor. It's not like she didn't know how to handle him.

Well, kinda…

Two hours later, Maggie was wiping off her hand from tossing the drink in the guy's face one last time.

"We really appreciate you coming back," Matt remarked as he looked at the footage from the take Maggie had just finished.

"Not a problem." Maggie smiled as she tossed the towel on the tray.

"I didn't want this scene to be cut, so I mean it." Matt turned from the screen to her. "Are you coming to the fundraiser? You know, it's to support keeping arts in schools."

Maggie's cheeks heated. "Yeah, I know. Danny mentioned it. I'm going to try my best to make it," she lied.

There was no way she was going. Danny told her the last one he went to had received over two million dollars in dona-tions alone. Everyone who's anyone was going to be there.

Which sucked for her. The nicest outfit she had in her closet was the black dress she wore to her grandmother's funeral. Even then, that was only a forty-five-dollar dress.

From what she understood the fundraiser was going to be

the event of the year. Like award-worthy event big. Maggie's forty-five-dollar dress was not going to cut it.

Plus, it wasn't that she didn't have a dress. She was sure Trevor was going to be there. She didn't need him singling her out and making rude comments in front of potential casting directors.

No, thank you.

"It's in the contract you signed," Matt continued. "Even though it was a small part all cast and crew are invited."

Maggie forced a smile on her face. "Thank you again. I really am going to try my best to make it."

"She'll be there, Dad," Danny announced, walking up to them. "You all set?"

Maggie bit her cheek to stop from blurting out *over her dead body.* Deciding to ignore Danny's comment, she looked back at Matt. "Yep. We just finished."

"Great. Sorry I wasn't around to see you throw the drink again. I needed to get some other things done with B-Crew. How was dinner with Lexi?"

"It was just what I needed. Thanks for giving her my number. We ended up at a hot dog place. Best damn hot dog I've ever had." She rubbed her belly. "I could have eaten ten of them."

Danny laughed. "If it's the one on Rosen, hell yeah. That place is legendary. The cook's a little weird. But the hot dogs make up for it."

Maggie instantly went into her impersonation of him. "Weird? You think I'm weird? You take this hot dog and you like it!"

Danny's eyes widened before he burst into a deep laugh. "Holy shit, Mags. That's impressive."

"Thanks." She smiled brightly at him as she shrugged. "It's a weird thing I do. I can impersonate people after watching them for a few moments."

"No shit. Really? Do me." The corner of his mouth turned up.

"No shit. Really? Do me," she replied, mimicking him exactly as he had done.

"Damn, I really am impressed."

"It's not that big of a deal." Her cheeks heated.

"Sure, it is. Why isn't that on your résumé? That could actually really help you."

"You think?" It had never occurred to her to add it. It was always just something dumb she did.

"Uhh, yeah. I mean an actor's résumé has a spot called 'special talent' what did you think that was?"

"I don't know. It's just something weird I do."

"Put it on there. Trust me."

"All right, fine I will," she said as she threw her backpack over her shoulder.

"I've gotta head back to the green room. Are you good to walk out on your own?"

"Yeah," she reassured him. "And, if I get lost I've learned my lesson on opening doors."

"Just text me if you get lost, okay?" A playful smile appeared on his face.

"Will do." She turned to head out the door. However, before walking out she turned back. "Lexi said something about us all hanging out sometime. Do you wanna hang out?"

Danny cocked his head to the side as he grinned. "For you two, I'm always free. Plus, Lexi is a fuckin' riot. She's amazing."

Maggie briefly looked him up and down. When he'd said Lexi's name there was something that flashed through his eyes. *Was there something between Lexi and Danny?*

Truth was, Maggie herself had gotten a girl boner every time she was with Lexi. She didn't know if it was from her stunning looks or her out-of-this-world coffee making ability.

Either way, she could see why Danny might like her. There was absolutely something there with Danny and Lexi, and she *was* going to find out what it was. "I'll text you later. See ya, Danny."

Maggie turned back to exit with a bounce in her step as she made her way to her car. "I wonder if Lexi likes Danny?" *Maybe Danny could ask Lexi to the fundraiser?*

Pushing the thoughts aside, she made her way to the car, throwing her backpack on the passenger seat before she got in. It was a hot day in L.A. and unfortunately, her car did not have working air conditioning. She rolled down the windows and hoped for the best. Putting her key in the ignition she turned it.

Turns out her air conditioning was not the only thing that didn't work.

"Come on. Please don't do this to me." She looked at the ceiling. "Universe, if you love me at all you'll have this car start."

She turned the key again.

Nothing.

"For fuck's sake!" She slammed her hand against the steering wheel in anger. When the horn went off she jumped. "Are you yelling back at me?"

"Are you talking to your piece of shit car or yourself?"

She looked up only to see none other than the bane of her existence.

TREVOR PULLED into the lot early. His call time wasn't until four but after his inopportune conversation with Lexi, he wasn't in the mood to go back home.

When he'd turned back after her last remark, she was

doubled over in laughter. Lexi was actually laughing so hard she snorted.

That just pissed him off more.

After calling her a bitch, he threatened to ruin her even if she did have the best damn coffee on the whole west coast, he then tried to leave. Before he could take a step toward the door though, she'd looked him up and down and accused him of having a chubby every time he saw Maggie.

At first, he panicked. How in the hell would she have known that? This had gone too far, and he was going to put a stop to it. Unfortunately for him, he forgot how ruthless Lexi really was. After arguing with her and failing miserably, which resulted in him walking out even more annoyed, she had the gall to holler at the top of her lungs, "Get it boy!" as he stormed out.

She wasn't getting a tip tomorrow. Nope. No tip for her!

On the drive to the set, he did everything he could to try and calm down.

Instead, he only got worked up more. Of course, Lexi would know his dick had caught some weird disease and responded whenever Maggie was around. Lexi fucking knew everything.

Great. Now that Maggie and Lexi hang out, the first thing probably out of Lexi's mouth would be how I get a chubby looking at the chubby girl.

"Fuck!"

Trevor turned down the road to the soundstage and groaned. "What the *fuck* is she doing here?" He was already agitated and now he was going to have to deal with her. *Great.*

He got out of his car and stormed over to where Maggie was parked, ready to give her a piece of his mind when he heard, "For fuck's sake." Maggie then slammed her hand down causing the horn to sound. She looked accusingly at her steering wheel. "Are you yelling back at me?"

Trevor chuckled then shook his head banishing the foreign emotions when it came to Maggie. He walked over to her window. "Are you talking to your piece of shit car or yourself?"

He watched as she looked at him, then dropped her head to the headrest and looked at the roof.

"Screw you Universe and all your cosmic universe-y shit you do. I must've really, really fucked up in a past life." Maggie turned to him. "What do you want, McCain?"

"Why are you here?" he asked, instantly going for the "show her you're pissed" demeanor.

"Going for a fucking stroll. What do you think I'm doing here, on a *film* set?" She got out of her car pushing him out of her way.

Trevor watched as she walked to the front of the car and popped the hood. "You know your car is a piece of shit, right? Is it even safe to drive?" he asked, walking to the front of the car to stand next to her.

Maggie narrowed her eyes at him. "A regular Sherlock Holmes, now aren't you?"

"No need to be snippy," he remarked. He was surprised when he heard the cheer in his voice. Although, he didn't understand exactly why he wasn't a fan of her driving around in this death trap.

"No need to be snippy? You're a piece of work, you know that?"

"From where I stand, *your* car is the one that needs work."

Maggie looked to the sky. "I know murder is wrong, but what if it's someone who really deserves to die?"

"Are you trying to murder me?" His hand shot to his chest.

"Trust me, if I was *trying* to murder you, you'd know it."

He ignored her as he looked at the engine. "What's wrong with this rust bucket that you call a car?"

"Don't you have somewhere you need to be?"

He was glad he was getting under her skin. "Not for another few hours." He shrugged. "That's enough time to watch you struggle for a while. I'm sure if I call Danny, he'd get me a chair and a drink."

She started to physically shake before she turned to him. When he saw the unshed tears in her eyes, he instantly felt like he'd been punched in the gut.

What the hell?

Why was his first reaction to bring her into his arms and tell her it was going to be okay?

"You know until a few days ago I thought you were the coolest guy. I had all of your movies, posters, hell I even had all the magazines that featured you. I thought you were so talented." She turned away and looked at her car. "Now," she said, looking back at him. "I just hate you."

Maggie moved to the passenger side of her car, as she retrieved her phone and punched in some numbers. "Hello. Yes, my car broke down." She talked while she started to pace. "Really? That long? Umm okay. I don't really have a choice now do I?" She moved to the front of her car again closing the hood as she listened. "And how much is that going to cost? Shit. Are you kidding me? That's freaking highway robbery."

Trevor didn't know what came over him but he jumped for her cell phone grabbing it out of her hand.

"Hey!" she yelled.

He disconnected the call throwing the phone back onto her seat. "You don't need to wait for them. I'll take care of it."

"The hell you will!" Her teeth clenched as she glared at him.

If he was easily intimidated he would have actually been worried. Thankfully, he wasn't. He knew she wouldn't do anything. Not to him. She was nothing but a mousy little girl, *trying* to act all big and bad.

Plus, she'd just admitted he was her idol. He smiled at that. Damn right he was her idol, he knew *no one* could dismiss him. He'd made sure to gloss over the part she said about hating him. In all honesty, he hated her too. *Kinda.*

"I will. Get your stuff. I'll take you home and call my guy to come get your car."

"Hell no!" she screamed. "Who the fuck do you even think you are?"

Trevor arched a brow at her. "I'm the guy *trying* to do something nice for you."

"No, you're the guy who makes fun of my weight and my acting. You're the guy that tries to cut me down every single time you're near me. What in the hell are you smoking to think I would actually get into a car with you? Not if my life depended on it." She reached into her car and grabbed her phone.

"If you pick up that phone I will place you over my knee and spank your ass." The second he realized the words were out of his mouth he froze. *What the fuck did I just say?*

Maggie stilled.

Great going, Trevor. Why the fuck did you say that? Now he had images of her laying across his lap, her ass in the air. Let's not forget that his poor confused dick took instant notice as well.

"I'd really kill you then," she sneered.

Might as well go for broke.

"I mean it, Maggie. You pick up that phone and I'll smack your ass here and now."

"If you even tried it, I would murder you."

When he saw the tears in her eyes again, he took a deep breath. Maybe a different tactic could work here. "You're right."

Her mouth fell open as she stared at him.

"I know in L.A. everything is more expensive than it needs

to be. My car guy is great, he won't overcharge you. Plus..." He looked down at his watch. "I have a few hours before I need to be here. I can take you home and make it back in time."

"What's in it for you?"

If I do this maybe, just maybe, you'll get out of my head. Plus, I don't think I'll ever be able to forget the tears you had in your eyes when you turned to face me. He cleared his throat. "I get to annoy you with my presence on the way to your place. That's enough for me."

Maggie looked at him, then back at her car.

She really had no choice but to take his offer. Well she did, she could always call Danny or Lexi, her new *best friend.* A part of him wanted her to think of those options, but for some strange reason, a bigger part of him didn't want her to realize that.

Trevor got his way when he saw her shoulders slumped in defeat. She grabbed her bag from her car and shut the door. Without saying anything else, she nodded.

An ear to ear grin appeared on Trevor's face as they walked through the lot to where he parked.

Chapter Eight

AS MAGGIE WATCHED out the window of Trevor's SUV, she still couldn't believe she *actually* agreed to get in the car with him.

Something was clearly wrong with her.

Maggie chanced a glance over at Trevor. He seemed agitated, his hands were tight against the steering wheel. Seriously, his knuckles were almost white.

What's his problem?

If he didn't want to take her home, what possessed him to insist on it?

Stupid, stupid man.

Maggie rolled her eyes. No, better yet, stupid her. She should have just waited until the tow company came.

When she heard him make a noise she snapped her full attention to him. "Really, if it's that big a deal just drop me off on the side of the road. I can walk from here."

"Not in this neighborhood," he growled, glancing at her briefly before turning his eyes back to the road.

"What do you mean not in this neighborhood? It's a nice

place." She looked out the window and mumbled, "stupid jackass," under her breath.

"You're kidding, right?" he said mocking her. "We just drove past a drug deal."

She turned to glare at him. "You don't know that."

Why did he always have to act like he was better than her? Not everyone had the opportunity to live in the nicer places around L.A. She barely got by with her apartment as it was.

Fuck Trevor and his judging, Mcjudging eyes.

"When you see one guy hand someone cash and the other guy hand back a little baggie of white stuff, I'm pretty sure it's safe to say it's a drug deal."

Prick.

"I'm sure you'd know," she mumbled.

"Excuse me?"

"Nothing," she snapped. "Take a right at the next street and my apartment is about three blocks down on the right."

He turned the blinker on. "Did you just say I do drugs?"

She shrugged.

When she chanced another glance at him, he was staring at her, his jaw tight and his eyes narrow. "God, you're a piece of fucking work," he said. "Here I am, taking you home after your piece of shit car breaks down, out of the kindness of my heart, might I add, and you have to be a bitch."

"I'm not—"

"I do *not* do drugs, little girl," he sneered. "Just because I'm known to party and have a good time, does *not* mean I fuck around with that shit."

At first, she was taken aback. Yeah, Trevor and her hadn't really seen eye to eye before, but she didn't expect him to get this upset about her jab. Maybe she shouldn't have said anything.

Screw that!

Yeah, he offered to take her home, but in the end, he's

nothing more than a high and mighty jerk. "That's not what the gossip sites say," she said, poking the beast.

"The gossip sites are fucking garbage. Sure, the sex parties have some merit, but—"

"You're a pig!"

He snorted with amusement, winking at her.

Maggie's mouth dropped. This guy was nothing more than a total dick. If he made one more jab about her weight, she was going to find the next sharpest item she came across and stab him right in his stupid, jerk face. "Fuck you!"

"No thank you," he said, before pulling over to the side of the road. He looked around, then back at her. "This the place?"

"Yeah," she said, opening the door. Fuck this guy. The first thing she was doing once she got into her apartment was to call the tow company and get her car towed. After today, she wanted to wipe her hands of Trevor McCain.

Maggie grabbed her bag and turned to mumble a "thanks", only to see the driver's side empty and Trevor making his way in front of the SUV to her side. "What are you doing?"

"This neighborhood is horrible," he answered as if that was the only explanation needed.

"No, it's not."

"Yeah, it is." He grabbed her backpack from her hands and swung it over his shoulder and started to the door of her apartment building.

"Have you lost your ever-loving mind?" She took off after him.

Trevor turned to her as he made it to the door. "How do you know that behind this door there isn't some gangbanger ready to jump out and take you?"

"Fat people are harder to kidnap," she remarked without missing a beat.

To her surprise, Trevor threw his head back and roared with laughter. "I do see where that could cause a challenge."

Maggie narrowed her eyes at him, but in all honesty, she wasn't upset. He'd just agreed with her. Plus, she was sure she'd get another opportunity to stab him for making a crack about her weight. When he opened his mouth, there was a ninety percent chance he'd say something to piss her off.

"Just give me my bag and go," she said, reaching for her backpack.

Trevor ignored her as he walked to the mailbox slots where he scanned the names.

Apparently, he was smarter than he looked. Maggie knew the second he found her name and apartment number. Turning from the slots he made his way to the elevator.

"Doesn't work," she said matter-of-factly.

"You have to walk up four flights of stairs every day and you're still..." He looked her up and down as he asked in disbelief.

"It amazes me that you haven't had your face rearranged. How is it possible you haven't gotten the shit beat out of you for the crap you say?"

"Everyone loves me." He moved past her taking the steps two at a time.

"Dick."

When they made it to her floor, he walked down the hall looking at the numbers on the doors. Once he made it to her apartment he waited expectedly.

What. The. Hell.

Maggie summoned everything she had inside of her to make it through the next few minutes. Closing her eyes for a moment she took a deep breath. *Universe, I know the past couple of days we've been having a lovers' quarrel. But I swear, if you continue to fuck with me, I will lose my shit! Just have him drop my bag next to the door and leave. That's all I'm asking.*

When she opened her eyes, she took the final steps to the front door noticing Trevor wasn't leaving.

Screw you, Universe, it's on!

She grabbed her keys from her pocket. She unlocked her door, before taking a deep breath and turned to him. "Thank you, Trevor. I appreciate the ride and the walk to the door. Although it was unnecessary, and I really should punch you for the words that come out of your mouth, I do appreciate it."

Trevor opened his mouth to say something when a loud screech came from inside her apartment.

Damnit!

"What the fuck was that?" he asked, moving past her right through her front door. "You got some freaky shit going on in here?"

As if right on cue, Pocket sang his "welcome home" song.

"Dear God, what the absolute fuck is that?"

Maggie closed her eyes and asked the Universe for strength. "That's my Siamese cat, Pocket."

"That is *not* coming from a cat. That sounds more like something dying."

Offended, Pocket came from around the corner and glared right at Trevor. He then opened his mouth and screeched again.

"Is it sick?" Trevor asked, staring at her cat concerned, and a little amazed.

"No, he's not sick. He's a Siamese. They talk." Maggie bent down to pick up Pocket. Cradling him in her arms she turned back to Trevor.

"YOU WILLINGLY GOT a cat that made that kind of noise, and you say something is wrong with *me?*" Trevor looked at the possessed creature Maggie had mistakenly called a cat. Sure, it looked like a cat, but no way in hell was that *thing* a cat.

"Something *is* wrong with you. There is nothing wrong with Pocket," Maggie defended.

"I beg to differ." Trevor looked around her apartment. It was small, it only had one other door leading to what he assumed was the bedroom. "Huh, when I pictured your place it wasn't so..." He struggled to find his next words. "*Normal?*"

Maggie snorted, rolling her eyes. "What did you think? I lived in some cardboard box?"

"I don't know, maybe something from the fiery pits of hell?"

Maggie laughed. "I don't even know what to make of that." She walked past him, and into the kitchen. Well, he assumed it was the kitchen. It had a fridge and a sink. But the word kitchen was stretching it. When she returned she held out her hand to him.

"Here's ten dollars for gas."

Trevor's eyes widened as he looked down at the cash. What a fucking insult. "I'm not taking your money."

"Take it."

"No."

The reality of being in her home was starting to get to him. He did the only thing he knew to get the upper hand once more. "By the looks of it, you need the money a lot more than I do." *I'm sorry.* His chest tightened as the words came out. What the fuck was his problem? He knew it was wrong. No one deserved that treatment. And yet he couldn't stop the words from coming out. *Wait, where in the world had that come from?*

Instantly Maggie's face hardened as her jaw tightened as her eyes narrowed. "Get out!"

"Jesus, your mood swings change faster than anyone I have ever met before."

"Are you fucking kidding me right now? You constantly insult me, and if anyone's mood changed in the blink of an eye, it'd be you," she snapped.

Surprisingly the cat—so she called it—was glaring at him. Its demeanor seemed to change as well. If he didn't know any better, he'd guess the cat was trying to plot his death. As if to confirm his suspicion, the cat slowly blinked staring at him with nothing but pure evil in its eyes. When the cat jumped from her arms, Trevor almost jumped back, frightened. Shaking his head to ignore the feelings–after all, it was just a cat—he said, "See this is what I'm talking about."

"I swear to the Universe above, if you don't get out of my apartment right now, I will kill you."

Something in Maggie's stare made Trevor believe her. He almost stumbled back. With all her talk of murder, he wouldn't put it past her. Just then to his dismay, he felt his lower half come to life.

Are you fucking kidding me?

Why is it every time she spat fire at him, his dick jumped to attention? Trying to figure it out, he looked her up and down. Her arms were crossed under her chest pushing her breasts up. He had to hold his groan in as he continued to peruse her body. Her left leg was a little in front of her right, her hip popped out clearly in annoyance. His eyes continued to trace the curve of her body. He had to fight the urge to reach out and grab onto her hips and bring her closer. "Fucking hell!" he hollered.

"Don't you yell at me, in *my* home. You're a bastard, Trevor. Now, get the hell out!"

Get out? That's exactly what he planned to do. She'd once again placed some of her weird fucking witchcraft on him and his poor unsuspecting dick.

The cat screeched again, making him jump. "What the fuck is wrong with that thing?"

"He's just like his Momma. He hates you."

At a loss for what to do, especially with his body acting insane, he fumbled. "Make sure I don't see you around anymore," Trevor growled, making his way to the door. "I've had enough of you."

"Right back at you, dickhead."

He turned and glared at her as he swung open the door and stepped through. "Make sure you lock the door."

He watched as her eyes widened for a moment before narrowing. "Are you threatening me?"

"No." His teeth clenched. "It's a bad fucking neighborhood. Lock the fucking door."

Trevor grabbed the doorknob and slammed it closed behind him. He stood there for a moment and waited holding his breath. Once he heard the lock, he finally made his way back down the hall. After jogging down the stairs and sprinting to his SUV he got inside and took a deep breath.

He was beyond pissed at himself. He had to reach down and adjust his pants. His dick was pressing so hard against the fly he almost couldn't drive.

What the hell is wrong with me?

After making room so his dick could breathe, he threw his SUV into drive and took off. Briefly, he looked in his rearview mirror as he sped away. Seeing the apartment building, his anger continued to rise. This was not a good area of town. Anyone with half a brain would know it wasn't safe. Especially, not if she lived alone.

Wait, did she live alone?

He froze as he thought back as he pictured the apartment in his mind. He didn't see any sign of someone else living there. It was a one-bedroom apartment, right?

She could have a boyfriend.

His hands gripped the steering wheel.

"*Boyfriend,*" he sneered.

Instantly, he pushed the thought out of his mind. Who the hell cared if she had a boyfriend or if she lived in a shitty part of town?

"Boyfriend." He laughed.

He continued the drive in silence for a few moments.

He felt his body tighten before he spoke his next words, "She better not have a boyfriend."

Chapter Nine

TREVOR WATCHED as Danny sat at the other end of the table eating his lunch. He was once again talking on his phone and Trevor knew exactly who he was talking to.

Glancing around he saw the cafeteria was practically deserted. He wasn't surprised. He knew the crew was already setting up for the next scene.

Normally, Trevor would have eaten his lunch in his trailer, but for some crazy reason, he had taken to eating with the crew. More importantly, anywhere near Danny.

The day after dropping Maggie off at her – was probably a murder scene once – apartment, he realized Danny talked to Maggie almost every day at lunch.

But the little rat still swears they aren't sleeping together.

Was Trevor stalking Maggie? No. He was just making sure she wasn't in any way going to be near him. Yup, that was exactly what he kept telling himself.

As Danny continued his conversation, Trevor could feel himself getting antsy. He pulled out his phone and checked his email once again. There was no new information on her car.

He made a mental note to call Bruce, his car guy, once they wrapped for the day.

When he left Maggie's apartment, he'd called Bruce, and had her car towed. Later that night, after Bruce finally had a chance to examine Maggie's car, he found out her car had more problems than it was worth to fix it.

Bruce suggested to scrap the car and get a new one. But Trevor wasn't having it. Something inside of him wouldn't allow it, knowing Maggie couldn't afford a new car.

In the end, he told Bruce to fix it no matter what the cost was. He was going to pay for it.

That was a fun conversation.

It ended with Trevor threatening Bruce if he ever told Maggie just how bad her car was and how much it would really cost to repair it, he'd ruin him. So, they came up with a plan of what Bruce was actually allowed to tell Maggie.

There were just some minor issues and it would only cost five hundred dollars.

Trevor wanted to pat himself on the back for coming up with such a good plan. Even if Bruce had his doubts. At first, Bruce argued that the time it would take to fix the car would give away the fact that the whole process would be more than a five hundred-dollar job.

In the end, though, they agreed to tell Maggie the shop was busy and that she should be able to get it back in a week or two. And, Bruce was under strict instructions to email Trevor with updates along the way.

Trevor wasn't surprised to find out Maggie had refused the loaner car. She was just that stubborn.

Stupid woman.

Whatever. He didn't care, he didn't even know why he was going through all this trouble to fix her car anyway.

Trevor closed his eyes and groaned. Yes, he did. He knew when Maggie first turned to face him, the tears he saw in her eyes tore him apart. Every night since then, whenever he closed his eyes it was all he could see.

"Are you planning anything for it?" he heard Danny ask. "Wait! It's the night of the fundraiser? Then you have to come so we can really celebrate."

Trevor continued to watch, trying to piece together what was being said on the other line.

"You only turn twenty-seven once. What better way to celebrate than by going to the hottest party of the year?" Danny argued.

Turn twenty-seven once? Was it Maggie's birthday?

"We can make a big to-do of it. Does Lexi know it's your birthday?" Danny laughed at the answer given over the phone. "I don't blame you. She'd probably go crazy and do something extravagant for you."

Trevor nodded. He knew that's exactly what Lexi would do. She was someone who seemed to thrive on special occasions like birthdays or Groundhog's Day.

"Damn straight, I'm telling her. As soon as I'm off the call with you, I'm texting her. Be prepared for the hurricane that is Lexi when she finds out you didn't tell her about your birthday."

Trevor grinned. He'd love to see someone else, especially Lexi, get on Maggie's case.

"No, Maggie, you and Lexi are *both* coming to the fundraiser. Especially now that it's on your birthday." Danny took a bite of his food. "Fine, we'll talk about it later. How's your car doing? Any new updates on when you will get it back?"

Trevor looked at his phone again. There better not have been any updates that he didn't know about. Especially, if he was the one footing the bill.

"That sucks, Mags. So, you haven't been doing anything? Not even auditions?"

She could be going on auditions if she wasn't so stubborn about the loaner car.

"At least it's not that expensive, right? It could be more than the five-hundred." Danny looked down at his watch before speaking. "Hey, Mags, I got to go. Good luck with Lexi tonight."

After hanging up the phone, Danny grabbed his plate of trash and made his way to the garbage. Quickly, Trevor did the same.

"Watch it," Trevor said purposely bumping into Danny.

"You bumped into me."

"Whatever, just watch where you're going." Trevor grabbed a bottle of water that was on the table next to them. "Interesting conversation you just had." He took a gulp of his drink.

"Were you eavesdropping?"

"Kinda can't help it when you talk loud enough for people to mistake you for using a bullhorn."

"You're ridiculous." Danny moved past him to start walking toward the next set.

Trevor quickly followed. "Is Maggie's birthday coming up?"

"Why do you even care?"

"I don't," Trevor said, willing his body to believe it. "It sounded like it was on the night of the fundraiser. So, she won't be coming now, right?"

"What is your problem with her? Yeah, she walked in on you, but it's not like she did it on purpose. Why do you have it out for her?"

"She threw a drink in my face and verbally assaulted me."

"So what?" Danny countered. "If it was that big of a deal to you then why did you take her home when her car broke down?"

Good question.

He was still trying to figure that out for himself. Along with paying for her car to be repaired without her knowledge. Oh, and let's not forget his newfound hobby of pretty much stalking her.

"I was trying to bank in the good karma. Trust me, I fucking regret every fucking moment of it." *Liar.* "Did you know she has this *thing* that she swears is a cat? Fuckin' thing is *not* a cat."

Danny's eyes widened. "You went into her apartment?"

Oh shit! Obviously, Maggie had left that detail out. Maybe if he ignored the question he could get out of this hole he just dug himself into.

Thankfully, his phone started to ring. Looking at the caller ID he saw Bruce's Auto Repair. "I have to take this."

Trevor answered the phone as he ran off through the lot, leaving Danny there still gaping.

UNIVERSE, why do you hate me?

"Jeez Lexi, yes, I'm sorry I didn't tell you I was having a birthday soon. I didn't think it was that big of a deal." Maggie tried to calm down her hysterical friend on the other line.

"Didn't think it was a big deal? Are you crazy? Of course, it's a big deal, it's your birthday!"

"Birthdays aren't that big of a deal to me. I only ever celebrated them with my Grammie." Maggie felt something inside of her break. She absolutely loved birthdays. However, when she was younger she realized her birthdays were just an excuse for her mother to throw some elaborate party that only benefited her. There had been more birthdays than not where her mother had "thrown her a party" but usually forget to get a cake. Maggie always ended up somewhere in the corner or told to make herself scarce.

When Maggie was sixteen her Grammie finally caught on to what her mother was doing, and instead of showing up to her mother's "planned party" her and Grammie would celebrated instead.

In actuality, Maggie loved birthdays, really truly loved them. But not this year. This would be the first year without her grandmother and she didn't feel much like celebrating. Besides, who would want to celebrate their birthday by themselves anyway?

"Lexi, it's really no big deal. I just recently found out the fundraiser was on my birthday, and I only told Danny so he'd understand why I couldn't go." In hindsight, it was a horrible idea to tell him. She still couldn't afford a dress. Even now more than ever with the five-hundred-dollar bill from the repair shop.

Thank the Universe it wasn't more than that. The five-hundred-dollar bill was already putting a huge dent in her pocket. But there was nothing she could do about it. She had to have a car. How was she going to get to auditions? What about a callback, or even to film, if she didn't have her car?

"Well, that was dumb! Of course, he was still gonna want you to go. Who else gets to celebrate their birthday while rubbing elbows with Hollywood elitists?"

"I know that now!"

"No need to worry, my sweet. Danny invited me to go as well so we can really *celebrate your birthday, together."*

"He asked you as his date?" Maggie smiled. She *knew*, deep down in her soul, there was something between Lexi and Danny. More on Danny's side than Lexi's but she had a feeling, Lexi did her best to hide her feelings, rather than embrace them.

"Sure did," she said. *"I think he had a sinking feeling that if I didn't go with you, you wouldn't have agreed to go."*

"I still haven't agreed to go," Maggie grumbled. Didn't these people understand she couldn't afford it?

"Well, what in the world is stopping you? For real, chica, this is gonna be your night to shine."

All she wanted to do was spend a quiet evening in, watching old horror movies. The ones her and Grammie used to watch all the time. She didn't want to be dragged out when all she wanted was to sit at home and cry about losing the only person that ever really loved her. "I just don't want to go. Okay?"

"That's not a good enough excuse there, missy."

"I can't afford it!" she yelled. "I can't afford a new dress, and the only dress I have is the one I wore at my grandmother's funeral. I don't have the money to get my hair and makeup done! And, everyone keeps pushing me to go, I just can't, okay?" She was panting when she finished her sentence.

"Oh, that's it?" Lexi asked, nonchalantly.

Maggie felt like she missed something in translation. *What the hell did she mean, "that's it"? Did everyone in L.A. have a Hollywood premiere dress, hairstylist, and makeup artist at the ready?* If Maggie wasn't feeling embarrassed and confused enough Lexi started to laugh.

"Maggie, love, I've got you covered. You've got some a-m-a-zing hips. I have dresses that would make you look hotter than any Hollywood starlet. Plus, if you haven't quite realized I love makeup and hair!"

Maggie didn't know what to say.

"I'm so excited!" Lexi shouted. *"Not only do we get to cele-brate your birthday we now get to hang out the* whole *day! Ohh, I know! We can do a mini-spa day in honor of your birthday. I have millions of nail polishes and thousands of face masks! Oh my God, Oh my God!"*

Maggie could picture Lexi dancing around. The girl was completely predictable when it came to that. Taking a deep breath Maggie tried to calm herself. She really had no excuses now, her dress dilemma had been taken care of, heck even her hair and makeup.

"Fine, Lexi, I'll go."

"*Yay!*" Lexi screeched into the phone.

After hanging up the phone with Lexi, Maggie sat on her couch and relaxed for a few minutes. Looking at her phone she went to her pictures and scrolled to her favorites folder. There in front of her were tons of pictures of her and her grandmother.

"Am I really going to do this, Grammie?" she asked, looking at a picture of the two of them.

She wasn't expecting a reply, but Pocket felt the need to answer her anyway with a loud screech.

"Man, Pocket, Trevor was right. You're so not a cat." She laughed. "Cats don't make that kind of noise."

She started to pet Pocket behind the ears when a thought came to her.

"Oh shit! Trevor was going to be there."

Chapter Ten

IT WAS WAY TOO hot for Trevor to be walking around L.A. in a hoodie, sunglasses, and jeans, but he had no other choice. If he wanted to stay out of sight and away from the crazy hordes of fans, he had to do everything he could to stay invisible.

Usually, whenever he needed to go out in public, he would have his assistant or someone else do it for him.

This time, however, it had to be him.

So, here he was walking around the streets of Los Angeles sweating his ass off. And, for what? He still couldn't believe he was actually doing this. What in the world had possessed him to even give a shit? Shaking the annoyance out of his head, he continued down the street looking for the perfect store. The problem was, he wasn't even sure what he even wanted to buy.

"This is stupid," he murmured, as he continued his never-ending quest down the populated streets of L.A.

Just then, his phone rang.

Looking down he couldn't help but smile. Hopefully, it would be good news. "Bruce," he answered. "How's the car?"

"Hey, Trevor, I'm calling to give you a quick update."

As Bruce went into the update on Maggie's car, Trevor spotted the store he wanted to go into across the street.

"Yeah, yeah, yeah. That's fine, whatever it costs," he said absentmindedly, as he looked both ways before crossing the street to the store. "When will it be done?"

"I got the last part in this morning. So, no later than this Wednesday—"

"Can't you see I'm fucking walking here!" Trevor hollered as he slammed his fist onto the incoming car that almost ran him over.

"Why don't you use a crosswalk, asshole?" the driver shouted back.

"This is L.A. No one uses crosswalks, you piece of shit! Now watch where you're driving." Trevor jogged to the other side of the street glaring at the car that dared to run into him. Before the driver was out of sight, Trevor flipped him the bird.

"Trevor, are you okay?"

"Yeah, I'm fine," Trevor answered, now annoyed more than ever. Why was he going through all this trouble to begin with?

"Okay, well, I'm gonna let you go. I'll call you on Wednesday to settle the bill or if anything else comes up."

"Fine."

Trevor ended the call and looked at the store. What the hell was wrong with him? Somehow his feet carried him right into the store.

"Hi," a sales clerk greeted him. "Is there anything I can help you with?"

Trevor looked her up and down. She was beautiful. Typical Hollywood beauty, she had bright blue eyes, bleached blond hair, a huge rack, and an even bigger ass. Sure, he could instantly tell they were all fake, but who was he to judge?

He scanned her body once more before landing on her face.

Nothing.

Not even an ounce of interest from his lower half. Taking a deep breath, he looked away from her and glanced around the store.

That's when he saw it.

Ignoring the clerk, he walked right over to the display case.

I'M GONNA KILL HER!

Maggie was over it. She was also now ninety-nine percent sure Lexi was the devil herself. Silly Maggie for thinking today was going to be a *fun* experience getting ready.

With Lexi in charge, she should have known better.

"No! Oh, hell no," Maggie shouted. "Have you lost your mind?"

Lexi stared dumbfounded back at her. "What do you mean *have I lost my mind*? It's a normal experience in a spa to get waxed there." Lexi moved back to the hot wax to stir it.

Okay fine, she had to agree that waxing was a normal thing at a spa, and she had given in and let Lexi wax her legs, but waxing her va-jay-jay? Hell no! No wax of any sort was *ever* going near there.

"I do it all the time," Lexi stated.

"TMI!" Maggie groaned as she moved away from her friend. "I let you wax my legs. What more do you want from me?"

"You're acting like it's a huge deal. It's not."

"I can't believe you even thought for a moment I would let you anywhere near my lady bits with hot wax. How do I know you won't burn me, or cause permanent damage?"

"Puhhlease." Lexi rolled her eyes. "I told you I've been waxing myself for years. Can you believe spas have the *nerve* to charge you sometimes seventy-five dollars just for a wax? It's freaking highway robbery. Us girls are supposed to look out for each other. Not try and rob us blind. I can do my whole body and yours for a third of that price. Plus, I didn't burn you when I did your legs."

"But, that's not my vagina. Not gonna happen, Lexi. You are not coming anywhere near my vagina with *hot* wax."

"But this is one of my birthday gifts to you! Trust me, there is no feeling like a freshly waxed hoo-ha," Lexi remarked. "I feel like I can take on the world. My confidence goes through the roof."

"It's already through the roof."

Lexi winked. "Exactly."

Maggie looked at the ceiling. "Universe, when I asked for friends, I meant normal ones." Maggie looked back at Lexi who had a stupid grin on her face. "You are enjoying this far too much."

"I'm enjoying the fact I get to hang out with my best friend on her birthday. I'm enjoying that said best friend and I are having a much-needed girly day together and then and only then, said best friend and I are going to the hottest party of the year."

"You only want to go to the party," Maggie protested, reaching for anything to stop this parade of craziness. When Maggie glanced at Lexi, she realized her mistake. Lexi looked downright appalled. Her mouth opened and closed like a fish out of water before hurt flashed through her eyes.

"I don't give a fuck about that party, Maggie. Parties come and go. What I care about is making your twenty-seventh birthday special. And let's not forget your first birthday here in L.A." Lexi turned away from Maggie and started putting away her waxing supplies.

Maggie instantly felt like an asshole. Sure, normally getting her va-jay-jay waxed was never even on her radar, but all Lexi was trying to do was give her a good birthday. And, she had succeeded so far.

Even though she'd been tortured with the wax on her legs, Lexi had gone above and beyond with making her feel beautiful and pampered for her special day. You can't help but love someone like Lexi. She truly only has good in her heart. She might do some crazy things and be out of this world eccentric, but Maggie loved that about her. Even if she was weird.

"I'm sorry," Maggie said. "It was wrong of me to say you were only doing all of this for the party."

"I couldn't care less about the party, Mags. I just wanted to help you *feel* beautiful and special on your big day. We've talked about it. You said you wished you possessed my confidence." Holding up her hand she stopped any protest. "And no, having my vagina waxed isn't the reason I have confidence. But, you're right, I should have never even suggested it."

"Lex," Maggie started softly. "You have no idea how much what you've already done means to me. I've never had a birthday like this. No one other than my Grammie has taken this much time to do anything for me."

Lexi's smile spread from ear to ear as her freshly highlighted blue and purple hair fell around her face. "I see so much in you, Mags. My goal today was to help unleash it. I'm sorry I went overboard."

"You didn't go overboard," Maggie was quick to rectify.

"Offering to wax your, as you like to call it, *lady bits* is a little much." She shrugged. "I just wanted to help you feel confident and I went about it the wrong way."

Maggie sat there staring at her friend, letting everything sink in. Right in front of her was someone she had all but known for only a few weeks, if even that, and she had done more for her than anyone else had ever done for her. Lexi was an honest, genuine, true soul. Someone she was glad to call her best friend.

"Let's do it."

Lexi turned back to her, her head cocked slightly to the left. "What?"

"You're right! I do want to feel confident. I've had some weird ups and downs recently and I want what you have so bad. You take your size and make it work for you. You're hotter than half the bleached blond bimbos here in Hollywood, and if waxing my, as you like to call it, *hoo-ha*, will do that, then so be it," Maggie said.

"Waxing won't make you confident," Lexi reiterated. "That comes from inside. I was only suggesting it, because, even though your confidence needs to come from inside of you, having your hoo-ha waxed definitely helps speed up the process."

Maggie laughed. "You are one of a kind, Lexi. Never change."

"Don't plan on it." She turned back to her wax. "Now spread 'em."

"Umm," Maggie panicked. "You know I think I changed my mind..."

Lexi turned back to her, the corner of her mouth turned up. "Don't be a baby."

Four hours later, Lexi was putting the finishing touches on Maggie's makeup. After the grueling – never to talk about again, if she ever comes near her with wax she will gouge out her eyes – waxing, Lexi had started manicures, followed by hair and now makeup.

Who would have thought it would take this long just to get ready? No wonder why celebrities hire professional teams for all of this.

"You're beautiful," Lexi sang as she finished her last swipe of the makeup brush.

Maggie rolled her eyes. "Laying it on there a little thick now, aren't we?"

"I call 'em as I see 'em, and you, birthday girl, are one hot mama." Lexi finished up with a soaking of what she called *setting spray* all over her face.

"Oh jeez, Lex, what the hell?" Maggie choked.

"Hush up, it will keep all the makeup in place."

"So you're saying I'll be beautiful for my funeral, 'cause I'm pretty sure I just drowned."

Lexi laughed. "You're so dramatic. Anyone ever tell you that you should be an actor? Oh, wait." She laughed.

"Lexi, what would I do without you?" Maggie threw her head back in hysterics.

"You won't ever have to find out now, will ya?" she answered, pulling her into a hug.

Maggie truly hoped that was true. She never had a friend like Lexi and she hoped that no matter where life took her, Lexi, would always be by her side. A friend like her was hard to come by. "I hope not."

"You won't," Lexi said before she moved over to her closet and pulled out a garment bag. "Now, I know you are a couple sizes smaller than me. But I think this might fit you. I picked it up a few years ago and unfortunately for me, it never fit. But, it was so pretty I could never throw it out. At one point, I was going to cut it up and make other clothes out of it." She turned to Maggie. "I'm so glad I didn't." Lexi unzipped the bag and Maggie felt her jaw drop. *Holy shit!*

"It's beautiful, right?" Lexi asked, eyeing the dress longingly.

"It's stunning. Wow."

"And you're gonna knock this dress out of the park!" Lexi squealed as she jumped up and down.

"You know what, Lexi?" Maggie asked, walking over to the dress to feel it. "I think you're right. I am gonna knock this dress right out of the park."

"That's what I'm talking about!" Lexi started dancing in a circle and singing at the top of her lungs.

Maggie looked the dress up and down a huge smile spreading across her face.

"Thanks, Lexi."

"Don't thank me yet," she said as she stopped dancing. "Now go get into that thing, the car will be here in an hour, and I still need to do my makeup and get dressed," Lexi said, shooing Maggie off to the other room with the garment bag in hand.

"Jeez, okay."

As Maggie closed the door, she could hear Lexi squeal with excitement. "I can't wait to see the look on Trevor's face when he sees you."

Maggie gulped.

Chapter Eleven

IT'D ONLY BEEN an hour since Trevor had arrived at the party, and he was already done. He hated going to these types of events.

All eyes were always on him and especially tonight.

Everyone, and he meant *everyone*, was questioning why he didn't show up with a date. What was the big deal? If he didn't want to have a date, he didn't have to. There was absolutely no rule that said he had to show up with arm candy draped across him.

He looked around the room again. *Where the hell was she?*

Trevor knew she was coming on the arm of *Danny*. He heard him talking about it *again* yesterday. He reached into his pocket to feel if the box was still there. It had become an unhealthy obsession for him to make sure he brought it along.

Just like every other time before the box glided against his fingertips, reminding him that he somehow had lost his sanity somewhere in the past few weeks.

"Danny!" He heard Matt holler. Trevor instantly turned to the noise. What he saw knocked the wind out of him.

On either side of Danny were Lexi and Maggie.

Trevor blinked a few times, trying to gather his thoughts.

Maggie was *stunning*. Actually stunning was an understatement.

Trevor felt his heart start to race as his hands started to sweat.

"You okay there, Trevor?" Matt asked, knocking on his shoulder. "You're sweating."

Trevor heard him, but couldn't reply. His mouth was dry, as he struggled to remember how to nod.

"Wow," Matt continued. "Cleans up pretty good now, wouldn't you say?"

Trevor watched as all three of them made their way closer to them.

Fuck. Has she always been this beautiful?

Maggie looked like a classic 1940's pin-up. She wore a deep-red, skin-tight hourglass dress that hugged every curve of her body. The neckline plunged well below her breasts, giving her one of the most impressive racks he had ever seen in his life. Her makeup was the perfect complement to her look. Deep, deep, red lips that beckoned him to taste. Her hair was swept to one side. His fingers itched to run through the loose curls.

She moved with such grace, that he was taken aback. *No, no, no! Do not think like that. Do not imagine peeling – yes, peeling, because that's the only way you would ever be able to take off a dress like that—the material from her body, as you kissed along her bare skin.*

Trevor's lower half rocketed to life. He looked at the front of his pants as he did his best to cover himself. "You betraying bastard!"

"Excuse me?" Danny asked as he stood in front of him and Matt.

"Yeah," Lexi remarked. "Who you callin' a bastard?"

"Ignore him," Matt remarked, holding back his smirk.

"You girls look gorgeous." Matt leaned in and kissed Lexi on the cheek before turning to Maggie. "Absolutely gorgeous." He pulled her into a hug.

"Dad," Danny mumbled. "My dates. Not yours."

"Thank you." Maggie smiled.

Trevor watched as Maggie's cheeks reddened. He could see the blush crept all the way down her chest. He had to close his eyes before he thought of just how far the blush went.

That was it. This was a horrible mistake. Instead of saying anything, he turned on his heel and left.

MAGGIE WATCHED as Trevor took off. Okay, so she wasn't quite sure how Trevor would react to seeing her at the fundraiser, but just outright leaving wasn't anything she pictured.

She looked down at her body. Maybe this outfit was a bad choice. Up until that moment, Maggie thought she looked drop-dead gorgeous.

Maybe not.

"Okay, that was uncalled for," Lexi announced from beside her.

Maggie shrugged. Who cares if he was *once again* going to be a prick? At least he didn't tell her she looked like a stuffed sausage or something. Especially, with all of these attendees around. "Who cares?" she mumbled as she looked to where Trevor had walked off.

"You really look unbelievable." Matt smiled at Maggie looking her up and down, taking her in.

"Thanks." She felt the heat rise in her cheeks again. This was the tightest piece of clothing she had ever worn in her life. And, she was certainly not used to all this attention.

"Nice shoes." Matt laughed.

Maggie looked down at her flats and laughed as well. They were the only thing Lexi couldn't stand about the outfit. There was no way in hell Maggie would have been able to wear heels. I mean she could have if she wanted to break her ankle in one point two seconds. Not the way she wanted to spend her birthday sitting in the E.R. "You gotta play to your strengths." Maggie shrugged with a smile.

"You know," Matt remarked. "I'm actually not surprised at all. I wouldn't expect anything less."

"I'm not sure if that's meant to be a compliment or not, but I'm going to take it as one."

"It is," he answered. He turned to Lexi and Danny started talking with them.

Maggie moved slowly to the side, away from the others as she took everything in. She'd seen pictures of parties like this on websites or on the entertainment shows late at night. But those photos did not compare to the real thing.

This was more extravagant than anything she had ever seen in her life. Where in the hell did people get the kind of money needed to pull off something like this?

"You're kidding me?" She heard Matt say. She turned to him as he pulled her into another hug. "Happy Birthday, Maggie. I had no idea."

"Oh." She blushed. "It's no big deal."

"The hell it ain't, sister," Lexi chimed in. "When are you going to accept that we are not letting your birthday go?"

"I didn't say anything," Maggie protested.

"Yes, you did." Lexi pursed her lips. "You acted like it isn't a big deal when it is."

"She's right," Danny agreed.

"I'm with them," Matt joined in. "How about this..." He turned and grabbed two glasses of champagne from a waiter who was walking past them. Handing one to her, he remarked, "We'll pretend this whole party is for your birthday."

"Oh no." Maggie threw her hands in the air. "We can't do that. This is for the kids."

"Well, you're younger than me, so that makes you still a kid." Matt beamed at his witty response.

"Exactly," Lexi said. "I love that logic!"

Maggie, not knowing what to say, decided it would be better to stay quiet. At this point, if she said anything to the contrary she'd probably have all three of them jumping down her throat. She held up her glass and plastered a smile on her face instead. Might as well give up.

"About time!" Lexi hollered as she turned on her heel to grab a champagne glass of her own her, then clinked it with hers. "Let's celebrate!"

Maggie couldn't help but smile. Lexi was one of a kind, and at this point, she wouldn't have it any other way.

WHOA!

This was way more than Maggie bargained for. They had been at the party for a little over an hour and a half. And, at this point, Maggie was done. Sure, the food was terrific, the drinks even better, but this wasn't her cup of tea.

Especially today.

She looked at the dance floor. Danny and Lexi were on a roll. They hadn't stopped bumpin' and grindin' for the last twenty minutes. The look on Danny's face was priceless, though. Lexi knew exactly how to get him out of his comfort zone, and boy was he ever.

Serves him right! Maggie watched Lexi dance around an awkward Danny. That will teach him to drag her to places she didn't want to go to.

Looking around the room, Maggie once again came up empty in her search for Trevor. She assumed he must have left.

After his abrupt exit when she arrived, she hadn't seen him. She shrugged. It was no skin off her nose.

Maggie took a deep breath and made her way out one of the side doors. She needed a few minutes of fresh air before she went back inside and dealt with hurricane Lexi.

Besides, this place was beautiful and who knew the next time she'd ever get to be somewhere this breathtaking again.

Maggie walked down the balcony and over to the railing. The night air had a chill to it, but it wasn't anything she couldn't handle. Maggie leaned on the railing and closed her eyes, breathing in the scent of the cool night.

So much had happened to her in just a few short weeks. She went from having a few lines in a movie to now being at one of the hottest parties of the year.

Maggie opened her eyes and looked out to the night sky. "Why does this feel like I'm doing this all wrong?" She crossed her arms over her chest. For the first time that night, she pushed aside her feelings and decided she would worry about it tomorrow.

"Hey."

Maggie's body stiffened as the voice carried to her ears. *Oh no!* Cautiously she turned only to see Trevor standing directly behind her. His hands in his pocket.

No matter the feelings she now held toward him, Trevor was still breathtakingly handsome. Even more so in his tailored tux. He might be a total ass, but he was a *hot* total ass. Doing a quick shake of her head, she pushed aside her inappropriate thoughts, she braced herself for the insults she was sure were about to come.

"A bit chilly tonight, isn't it?"

He shocked her with his normal small talk.

Okay, what's his game here? She eyed him as she tried to figure it out. "Yeah," she replied. "It's a little weird that there's a chill in the air."

"It happens from time to time at night. Have you ever been to Vegas? It's hot as balls during the day, but the night can freeze 'em off."

Maggie watched as he moved closer to her before leaning against the railing. "No, I've actually never been anywhere other than here and Florida. Where I'm from."

"Oh, well, if you ever get to go, just prepare yourself for that."

"Noted." Not knowing what to do, Maggie leaned against the railing again. *Well, this is awkward.* She chanced a glance at him only to see him staring out into the night. Okay, this was really weird. Maybe she should make her way back to the party.

As Maggie moved back on her heels to stand upright Trevor turned to her.

"I heard it was your birthday."

Maggie's eyes widened. *Oh no, this was it. This is where he was going to do something to humiliate me.*

"I overheard Danny mentioning it the other day," he continued. "Other people might think it's fun to go to these parties, but it's really not. It's more work than anything else. If it were my birthday, I would have told everyone to fuck off. There are probably a million other things you would want to be doing."

Maggie swallowed hard at his words. Where was this coming from? She was used to jerk Trevor, not whatever the hell this was.

"I mean, it wasn't my first choice of things to do." She crossed her arms over her chest. She could swear she saw heat in his eyes as he briefly looked down. *Not possible.* She must be losing it. "But it is kinda cool to say I've been to a party like this. Who knows when I'll get another chance or if I ever will."

"You will."

Now Maggie knew she was in some sort of alternate

universe. She looked at the sky. *Universe, what did I do now? Wait, am I even really here? No, I've probably passed out on the waxing table after Lexi ripped, what I'm pretty sure was my clit from my body. Yep, I'm experiencing some weird hallucination.*

"Anyway," he continued. He pulled his hand out of his pocket and handed her a small box. "You're not doing this the wrong way, by the way. You've just lucked out. Happy Birthday, Maggie." With that, he placed the box in her hand and took off.

Maggie froze, completely shocked at what had just happened. After a brief second, she looked at the box in her hand then back to Trevor making his hasty exit.

Carefully she slowly opened the box as her heart sped up and her hands began to shake. Lifting the top off, she saw by far the most beautiful necklace she had ever seen in her life. A silver chain with a diamond star pendant.

It was absolutely breathtaking.

Maggie quickly placed the lid back on the box and started to run in the direction that Trevor ran. "Wait!"

Chapter Twelve

SHOVING the box the best she could into her chest, Maggie took off in a jog, searching everywhere for Trevor. She made her way to the dance floor as her eyes continued to scan the room.

Nothing.

A deep growl escaped her lips. Her body was on high alert as she tried to make sense of what had just happened.

Why in the world had Trevor given her a birthday gift? A. Freaking. Birthday. Gift.

Not only that, but he was actually extremely nice to her. She was definitely in some alternate universe or something. "Oh God, he's probably sick and dying." Maggie felt a rush of urgency run through her. Scanning the crowd again, she saw Danny and Lexi still dancing.

With her targets now acquired she pushed her way through the crowd. Unfortunately, for her, when she set her sights on something she saw nothing else. That included the waiter with a tray full of hors d'oeuvres.

Within seconds, Maggie was on the floor with the waiter on top of her, apologizing profusely.

"Crap, ma'am, I'm so sorry. I didn't see you there," the waiter remarked as he stood. To her mortification, he grabbed the napkin that was on his arm and started wiping her down. "Please, I am so, so, sorry. I honestly didn't see you." The kid looked terrified.

Maggie looked at the waiter with horrified eyes as she reached out to stop his groping. "It wasn't your fault," she assured him.

Maggie looked around her, only to feel her stomach bottom out. The party had frozen and all eyes *and* cameras were on her. She turned to see Lexi and Danny making their way over to the scene of the crime. *Oh, God, could this get any worse?*

"Are you okay?" Danny asked, as he pulled her away from the waiter and into his arms. "You fell kinda hard."

Maggie glanced around as she continued to feel every eye in the room on her. "I'm fine, I'm fine," she whispered as she tried to get out of his hold.

Crap on a cracker. This wasn't good. Whatever, she couldn't think of the consequences right now anyway. She was on a mission and she wasn't going to let one of her clumsy occurrences stand in her way. Or, you know the fact that by tomorrow morning there was bound to be an internet video posted with the headline, "Fat chick was so hungry she jumped a waiter only for him to grope her". She inwardly cringed. *Nope! You can deal with that tomorrow, Mags, right now you have to find Trevor.*

"I really am fine." Maggie grabbed Danny's hand and dragged him through the ballroom, Lexi hot on their tail.

Maggie did her best to ignore the comments and whispers she was hearing all around her. *"Who does she think she is?" "Why is she even here?" "Who invited her?" "Did you see the way she jumped on the food?"*

Maggie mustered all the courage she had inside of her to

the surface. Once they all had made it through the double doors she turned to a very shocked Danny. She felt all her adrenaline coursing through her body as she started to shake uncontrollably.

"Babe, you okay?" Lexi asked, concern marring her face as she moved closer to her.

Ignoring Lexi, Maggie looked Danny right in the eyes. "I need you to tell me where Trevor lives and *now*."

"What?" Danny's face scrunched.

"You heard me," she repeated. "I need to know what Trevor's address is and I need it now."

"Oh shit, Maggie what did he do?" Danny looked at her with such concern that her body actually started to relax.

"Did he hurt you?" Lexi questioned. "I'll kill him."

Turning away from both of them, she started to pace while she tried to get her emotions under control. Closing her eyes, she took a deep breath. *So, I know your most favorite game is the Screw with Maggie Game, Universe, but right now, just this once please, I am begging you, give a girl a little break.*

She stopped pacing and turned back to them. "I need to talk to him. It's important."

"Okay," Danny said, "I can have his assistant—"

"No," Maggie interrupted. "I need you to tell me his address." She reached into the top of her dress, thankful the tumble with the waiter hadn't caused her to lose the necklace. Opening it she showed both Lexi and Danny. "He shoved this at me and took off."

Lexi reached out her hand to touch the pendant but something inside of Maggie snapped and she closed the box before Lexi could take it. The idea of someone else touching something that Trevor had given her nearly made her sick to her stomach. *Huh? No, it wasn't that. It's all the stuff that's happened in the past five minutes. My stomach is throwing in the towel.*

"Whoa…" Lexi's eyes shot back to Maggie. "Got ya loud and clear, sister, no one touches your love charm."

"It's not a love charm!" Maggie growled.

"Uh," Danny spoke, shock written all over his face. "So, Trevor just handed you this and took off? He didn't say anything?"

Maggie looked at both of them. Why can't people just listen to her for once and do what she asked? Taking another deep breath trying to control herself. "No, he said, 'Happy Birthday' and then took off."

"Right on!" Lexi exclaimed.

"No, Lexi, no 'right on'. Right now I need to talk to him."

Danny looked around a little weary. "I really can't give you his address," he remarked, apologetically. "It could cause so many problems and I'd probably lose my job… my career."

Maggie felt her world start to crumble. She was about to plead with him when Lexi spoke up. "Pish posh." Lexi beamed as she took hold of Maggie's hand and started to lead her out of the building. "You don't work for years and *years* in an exclusive neighborhood without finding out a few things." She winked at her. "I'll take you to him."

Thank you, Lexi!

As they made their way to the taxis, Maggie heard Danny sigh as he caught up with them. "Neither one of you drove," he reminded them.

"That is not a problem, my good man," Lexi chirped with excitement as she pointed to the line of taxis waiting.

Lexi's pure excitement of the situation started to cause Maggie's nerves to get the better of her. What was she doing? Why was Lexi so happy about it? She didn't like that Lexi was getting so much enjoyment out of her humiliation. She was going to have a serious sit-down talk with her once she figured this whole Trevor thing out.

"That's not what I'm saying," Danny remarked, he then spun them in the direction of his car.

What in the world did I just do?

Trevor threw his keys into the bowl by the door and then his suit jacket onto the back of his living room couch.

He had absolutely lost his freaking mind.

Walking to his kitchen he pulled open his liquor cabinet and reached for his favorite whiskey. Grabbing one of the glasses he poured himself a generous amount. Without a second thought, he downed it.

What the hell was so special about Maggie that he couldn't seem to get his shit together when he was around her? And, what a fucking loser move to throw her gift at her and then fucking take off like some scared little boy that just told his crush he liked her.

"*Oh, God,*" he groaned. He did *not* just do that.

Trevor couldn't stand Maggie. She was loud and annoying, didn't take direction for shit, and she was *not* his type at all. No fucking way. Sure, her tits were more than a handful which, if you asked him, he liked a lot. Her hips were big, but then again, they would fit perfectly in his hands as he pounded into—

"Fuck!" Before he knew it, the glass was flying through the room. When it hit the wall across from him, it shattered.

Ignoring the mess, Trevor walked back to his living room. Loosening the tie from around his neck, he undid the top few buttons of his shirt.

He had so many emotions running rampant through him, he didn't know what to do next. Pulling out his phone he scanned the numbers looking for a willing body. He knew he needed to get rid of all this pent-up energy, and what better way than to fuck it out? He mentally patted himself on the back. Not only would he get laid, but he'd also be wiping away the thoughts of Maggie from his mind.

Yep, this was exactly what he needed to do.

As he looked through the numbers, no one was catching his eye. Trevor paced the room as he felt his heart race. "Fuck, you are so fucking stupid. Why would you even give her that necklace?"

Trying his best to wash away the events of the night, he closed his eyes. He was going to randomly call someone and forget this night ever happened. That's when he felt his phone vibrate.

When he looked at it he saw he had a new text from a buddy of his on the crew.

You left too early, man. You missed a great show! Check out the video:

Trevor stopped pacing and leaned against the back of his couch thankful for the distraction. His heart rate picked up when he realized the video was of Maggie falling to the floor with a waiter on top of her.

Instant panic washed over him. *Was she all right? Holy shit. She fell really hard. Did she need to go to the hospital? What hospital is close for them to take her to?*

His mind raced as he tried to calculate what hospital to go to. His body relaxed as the video played out as he saw the waiter stand before pulling Maggie to her feet.

Out of nowhere jealousy shot through him. Someone else touched her. Not only that, the waiter practically groped her in front of *everyone.*

Trevor squeezed his phone in his hand, his anger taking over. *He's dead.* Throwing the offending object across the room, he heard the telltale sign of the screen shattering.

No one touches her!

Trevor looked at his keys in the bowl by his front door.

He snatched them from the bowl, ready to go kill the waiter, and then find Maggie. Keys in hand, he ran to the door.

Before he reached his front door he heard knocking.

Angry knocking.

Who the fuck would come to his house and then have the balls to try and beat down his fucking door?

That only pissed him off more.

Right now, he had something he needed to do and he had zero time for this bullshit. He swung open the door ready to pound the daylights out of whoever was there, only to be shocked by what he saw.

Chapter Thirteen

MAGGIE STARED into the shocked face of one Trevor McCain.

I mean honestly, she'd be shocked too if she'd shown up unannounced on someone's doorstep like this.

Wait, no. Hold up. There was no reason for this egotistical jerkwad to be shocked. Did he really think she wasn't going to go after him? He must be crazier than she thought.

Without a second thought, Maggie stormed past him and into his living room. Briefly looking around, she couldn't help but be impressed. For some reason, she had imagined his living space to be a dingy bachelor pad, but it was actually designed in a modern chic sort of way.

He had big leather couches that anyone would die to fall into and be enveloped in. Dark hunter green walls and an entertainment center that was so big, it should be illegal.

"Who the hell do you think you are barging in here?"

"Who do I think I am?" She spun to face him her hands on her hips, ready for battle. She was ready to fight and the gloves were coming off.

"Yeah, that's what I said." He sauntered toward her,

causing Maggie to take a step back. His eyes held something she hadn't seen before.

Scary man charging. Abort, abort!

"You don't get to show up at *my* home banging on the door as if you're trying to wake the dead," he growled.

"I wasn't waking the dead—"

"And another thing, who the fuck even told you where I live?" His nostrils flared as he took one last step in her direction.

Maggie looked into his narrowed eyes, and she saw nothing but anger. Why the hell was he angry?

He shoved a box in her hand and took off.

He's the one who constantly bullied her.

And for fuck's sake, he is the one that confused the hell out of her.

This was her last straw and she couldn't take it anymore. She should have never come to Hollywood. She should have stayed back home in Florida and figured something out. Because this... none of this was worth it.

She reached into the top of her dress and pulled out the box. "What is this?"

Trevor glared at her, before jerking his head away. "Fuck me, I should have known better."

"Excuse me?" Her brows shot to the ceiling.

"It's a gift," he mocked like she was a two-year-old.

"Don't you dare talk to me in that tone of voice." She stomped the rest of the way to him, poking him in the chest with her finger. "I know it's a *gift*. You yelled Happy Birthday and threw the box at me then took off. Why?"

"I don't know why you even care." His jaw was tight as he peered down at her.

"What is that even supposed to mean? I swear I need a freaking manual for you."

Then out of nowhere, realization hit. She threw her hands

over her mouth as she let out a tiny gasp. He'd only ever do this to make up for all the shit he'd done if he was dying. "Oh no, you really are sick. Are you dying? Have you told anyone? Are you sick right now? Can you stand? Do you need my help?" She placed the back of her hand on his forehead to check his temperature.

Trevor hit her hand away, taking a step back from her so he was no longer in her reach. "I'm not sick, you psycho."

"I'm not the psycho. You're the one that's dying and finally grew a conscience for the way you've been treating me. You're the psychotic person here, not me."

"It obviously didn't mean anything to you since not ten minutes later you were letting some guy practically fuck you on the dance floor," he growled deep in his throat almost scaring her.

"What are you even talking about? I wasn't on the dance floor at all except when—" She narrowed her eyes at him. "Are you talking about the waiter that *knocked me over* and was trying to help me?"

Trevor huffed as he rolled his eyes. "Oh, he looked like he was helping you all right. I could practically see how hard your nipples were and I was just watching a fucking video of it."

Maggie motioned to her outfit. "Do you see all this, numb-nuts? He was trying to help clean up all the shit that he spilled all over me. I swear to everything in the world, you seriously have something wrong with you."

Trevor took a step toward her forcing Maggie to move back. "You're right, I do have something absolutely fucking wrong with me. You wanna know what that is, Maggie?" he asked as he pushed her up against the wall.

"An STD?"

He growled so loud it caused her to shake.

Was it fear or anticipation? She didn't know.

"You," he answered. "You're what's wrong with me. Ever

since that fucking day you walked in on me, you've been the problem. You're the fucking cause of all my problems!"

Maggie's anger flared. *Fuck this guy!* She placed the palms of her hands on his chest and pushed as hard as she could until she freed herself from his confinement. "You fucking prick. You no good, low life, piece of shit! I'm not the cause of any of your problems. Funny enough, *you're* the cause all mine."

Maggie stormed past Trevor and headed toward the door. "I don't know why I even came here."

"To annoy the fucking shit out of me," he barked, glaring her way. "Admit it, you found the perfect excuse to stalk me, right? Now you know where I live. You don't have a car right now cause it's still in the shop so let me guess who dropped you off? Don't worry though, Maggie. Come tomorrow morning your precious boyfriend will be out of a job *and* a career."

Maggie swung toward him. "Danny didn't tell me where you lived, jackass! Something is so fucking wrong with you."

"Yeah, we've established that. My problem is *you.*"

Maggie stared at him as she tried to make sense of any of this. Why would anyone in the world act like this? He was nothing more than a spoiled child.

As she was contemplating finding the nearest object and tossing it at his head, what he said dawned on her. "How do you know my car is still in the shop?"

Maggie saw a brief second of panic play across his features, but he quickly recovered. "It's a piece of shit car. Of course, it's still in the shop."

"Yeah, but it's been *weeks.* How would *you* know it's still in the shop?"

"Lucky guess." He shrugged.

"No there is no lucky guessing here. You knew *exactly* where my car was. There was not even a hint of doubt in your words."

Trevor turned away from her moving throughout the room.

That only pissed her off more. *That jerk did not just dismiss me!*

Maggie stomped toward him, a new determination in her stride. When she stood directly behind him she pushed is back. "Answer me!"

When he didn't react, Maggie pushed him again. "Answer me, you jerk. How did you know my car was still in the shop? Are you the one stalking *me?*"

Trevor snapped toward her, pure hatred in his expression. "I know your fucking shit car is still in the shop because *I'm* the one who's paying for it!"

Maggie fell backward as his words hit her like a punch to the stomach. "What?"

Trevor took another step advancing on her. "You heard me. I'm paying for the repairs on your car that really needed to just be junked in the first place."

"You can't be the one paying for my car." Maggie shook her head in disbelief. "I already gave him a check."

"Jesus man, you're not only stupid, you're naïve as well. Who in their right mind would think all the shit wrong with your car would only be five hundred dollars? Especially in Los Angeles?"

Oh God!

Maggie's eyes widened, larger than she thought possible. He knew exactly how much she had paid the shop.

Her stomach bottomed out. Had he been controlling her this whole time? Was this some sick game to him? Maybe he was going to have her car fixed up and then make her indebted to him? Oh no, she could not have that. *No way!*

"You did this so I would have to owe you, didn't you?"

"You have got to fucking be kidding me!"

"You did! Admit it! This would be the perfect game for

you, fuck with my only transportation." Her fists clenched at her sides. "No transportation means no auditions, no jobs, no fucking money. I said I was sorry, okay? I swear I never meant to walk in on you with that woman. This is not the ultimate payback."

Maggie watched as confusion entered his eyes, but it was quickly masked with disappointment.

"You know what, I did it to be nice. Lord fucking knows why, but I did it 'cause I knew you needed to have a reliable car in L.A. Why can't you just be grateful that I helped you?"

"B-be grateful?" she stammered. "You want me to be grateful? I never asked you to help me with my car. Just like I never asked you to publicly humiliate me in front of the whole cast and crew." Her heart was about to explode out of her chest. "Oh wait, that's it now. You feel guilty. Hey well, at least you have some sort of a conscience in your delusional self-absorbed head."

"There you go again. Can't you just be happy with the fact that your car is getting fixed? You're such an ungrateful bitch."

"And you're a pompous fucking asshole that only wants to fuck with my career. I know you, Trevor. I've had to deal with people just like you my whole life. You think you're the first person to *fuck with the fat girl* just to get their kicks? Well, I have news for you. I've been dealing with bullies like you my whole fucking life. You're a walk in the fucking park compared to my own goddamn mother. So, you know what, Trevor. Take your fucking charity and stick it right up your fucking ass!"

Maggie stormed through the front door slamming it shut before heading out to the parked car where Danny and Lexi waited.

"Fᴜᴄᴋ!" Trevor paced around the front room trying to make sense of what had just happened. When he saw it was Maggie at his front door he lost his mind. All he could see is the image of that waiter's hands all over her. Something inside of him snapped and instead of doing what he originally planned, he lost it.

He fucking lost it.

And to make matters worse, she was still wearing the skin-tight dress. The same skin-tight dress that would be forever burned in his mind.

"Damn it! Fuck! Shit!" He continued to pace around the room. Why couldn't he get it together? He had planned on fucking up that waiter and then finding her, making sure she was okay and then... well, he didn't know what, but when she found him first, all his plans went to hell. It was like he got around her and all his common sense just disappeared.

And he insulted her, *again*. Why the hell did he keep doing that?

Trevor needed to get his shit together. There was no other way around it.

He closed his eyes and took a deep breath trying to control himself. Unfortunately for him though, the moment his eyes shut, images of her bouncing around angry as she stomped toward him clouded his mind. Her breasts bouncing, begging for him to reach out and touch them.

Fuck me.

Then the stupid image of the waiter's fucking hands all over Maggie's body shot through his mind.

Trevor snapped his eyes open, ready to murder. However, before he could do anything his eyes found the box he'd given Maggie on the floor.

"Fucking, brat!"

Trevor snatched up the box and headed through the front door.

Chapter Fourteen

MAGGIE SLAMMED the front door behind her after Danny and Lexi dropped her off. She was still so angry. How dare he accuse her of practically having sex on the dance floor! Fuck him.

All Maggie wanted to do was find out why he'd given her the necklace in the first place. But no, he had to go all crazy again.

And, then... freaking *then,* finding out he was paying for her car? What a load of—

As if on cue Pocket made an appearance as he came around the corner screeching at her. "Dear Lord, Pocket. Do you have to yell so loud? Can't you see Mommy's angry or at least sense it? Don't animals have that sixth sense?"

In true Pocket form, the cat blinked slowly at her, judging everything she was doing.

"Figures." Growling with frustration Maggie ignored her cat and stomped to her bedroom. She threw off her shoes, tossing them in different directions not caring where they landed. She then pulled out the pins in her hair and used her fingertips to massage out her hairdo, enjoying the feeling of her hair being free. When she was done, she tossed her long locks through the air. "That's better."

Maggie looked at herself in the mirror and sighed. Her hair was a mess now, which was fitting seeing as her dress had food all over it still. How did it come to this? How had one role in a film ended with her here? Standing in front of her mirror with her whole life spiraling out of control.

If only her grandma were still alive. She'd know exactly what to do.

Maggie let out a small chuckle as she shook her head.

Grammie would have given her a shot and told her to put on her big girl panties and kick some ass. Tears welled in her eyes as she looked at herself in the mirror. *I miss you, Grammie. I need you now more than ever.*

She pushed those thoughts away deciding it was better to not end the night in a crying mess as she reached behind her looking for the zipper on her dress. After what felt like a deep-sea search for treasure, she finally grabbed a hold of it.

Maggie started to pull it down, only then to realize her dilemma.

"Shit."

Unless she had arms like an alien that can magically elongate, there was no way this zipper was going to go all the way down. Instantly, she started spinning in circles, like a dog chasing its tail trying to lower the zipper.

When spinning failed, she started jumping up and down. "What the hell? Come the freak on. I don't want to die in the fucking thing." With jumping and then spinning not working Maggie decided to combine the two. "Why the fuck do they make dresses you have to have someone else take off for you? That is the stupidest thing ever."

"That's exactly why they make dresses like that," a deep hoarse voice answered. "Those types of dresses are only for the *start* of a night."

Maggie screamed at the top of her lungs as she spun around only to see Trevor leaning against her bedroom door-frame, Pocket at his feet.

"What the hell are you doing here?" She didn't know whether she'd entered some hallucination from spinning or if he was really standing there. Either way, she was pretty sure she was seconds from having a heart attack. Quickly she threw her hand over her heart. Her breath was already ragged from the exertion trying to get out of the dress. Having Trevor scare the beejeebers out of her, did not help. Once she got her breathing under control she narrowed her eyes at him. "How in the hell did you get in here?"

Trevor pushed off the frame and walked to her. "I knocked on the door and might I add knocked *loudly*. You didn't answer. I knew you were here so I tried the handle. I'm not surprised it was unlocked. You seem to be painfully unaware of your own safety."

"Excuse me?"

Pocket screeched in his own protest.

"Jesus!" Trevor looked down at the cat.

"Leave Pocket alone!" She poked Trevor in the chest.

"Why does it do that?"

"He's just like his momma. He doesn't like egotistical jerks breaking into his home and then insulting the person that feeds him tuna."

TREVOR WATCHED as Maggie stood there glaring at him with a fire in her eyes that only ignited him further.

Let her glare.

This was all her fault anyway. If she had never walked into his life, he'd be out fucking some random model right now.

But, no. Instead, he was here wanting to rip out his hair. And rip her out of the fucking dress.

After knocking loudly on the door, he tried the handle and was surprised when it opened. Then anger rolled over him. Didn't she know this wasn't the best part of town? Hadn't they already had that discussion? He pushed through the door, turned, and locked it. When he looked around, all he saw was the *thing* she called a cat.

The slow blinking really creeped him out.

When Trevor heard grunting come from the other room and what sounded like a commotion, he followed it.

However when he got in the bedroom, the sight before him nearly knocked him flat on his ass. Maggie was jumping around in a circle with her hands behind her back, grunting and moaning.

The sight of her chest bouncing felt like a punch to his gut. Any second now, those more than a handful globes would slip out of that dress and give him the show he'd been dreaming about.

That dress... that damn dress he knew she wasn't wearing a bra with. How could she? It plunged so low and was so tight she'd never had fit one on.

Doing his best to keep himself in check he looked down at the screaming four-legged creature. "How do you know that's what it's saying? What if it's really siding with me and calling you an idiot for leaving your door unlocked while you jump around with your tits out asking for *anyone* to walk right in and take whatever they wanted."

The *thing* screeched again causing him to jump.

"I know exactly what he's saying. *I'm* his Mom. Not you, numb-nuts!"

Trevor growled as his dick tightened. Why in the hell did her sass turn him on? When he first saw her bouncing around, his blood migrated south. Seeing her spit fire at him now had his dick straining against his zipper, trying to break free. He was sure it was leaving a mark on his skin.

Trevor took a step closer to Maggie, his eyes locked on hers. "Doesn't matter. *You* need to care about your safety. I shouldn't be able to just walk right in."

"Even if the door was unlocked you *still* shouldn't have just walked in here, you jerk!" She took an angry step toward him making them only inches apart.

God, he fucking loved that she never backed down. Even when he would try and use his size to intimidate her, she'd be right there matching him step for step.

He couldn't get enough. Maybe that's why he was always an ass to her. He wanted to see this side of her any chance he got.

She poked him in the chest. "And what gives you the right to pay for my car repairs?"

Trevor growled deep in his throat as he took a small step closer. This woman, this curvy, loud-mouthed, pain in his ass, beautiful woman was going to be the death of him.

"I have every right to pay for the repairs. I would have bought you a new fucking car if I knew you would have taken it. But, let's be real. We both know you're too stubborn for that." As he looked down on her, the passion in her eyes nearly unmanned him. Fuck. Why did she get to him so bad?

"You have absolutely zero right to do or buy anything for me! Until the event earlier, you've been nothing but a complete asshole to me."

"I took you home."

"Once! And you insulted me!" She glared at him. "Do you think insulting and humiliating me makes you a *nice* guy? Did you get dropped on your head when you were a baby?"

His dick jumped at her words and she spit more fire in his direction.

"And no, you have no right to do anything for me." Maggie snapped her hands on her hips.

Instead of taking her bait, Trevor looked her up and down, the red on her face had now colored her chest. Fuck him. He couldn't help but wonder if the blush went all the way to her nipples.

His dick jerked again.

Trevor's eyes moved back to Maggie's face as he honed in on her lips as he snapped. "I have every right. And do you want to know why?"

Trevor didn't wait for her answer. Instead he cupped her face in his hands. "I take care of what is *mine*." At his words he slammed his lips down to hers.

Chapter Fifteen

FUCK, *Maggie was perfect.*

Her lips were everything Trevor had imagined them to be and more. Silky and smooth. Like he was fucking kissing a cloud. How was that even possible?

Trevor reached behind her moving his hands to her ass so he could pull her closer to him as he shamelessly ground his dick against her stomach, not giving a fuck that the action made him look like an eager teenager.

Right now, he had one goal in mind. Fulfill every fucking fantasy he had about her.

"Trevor," she moaned into his mouth as she pushed closer to his chest.

"That's right. Say my name, Maggie." She was setting him on fire, he didn't know how much longer he would be able to hold on. The moment she started to grind her hips against his, he nearly snapped. He couldn't get inside of her fast enough.

As Maggie's hands moved up his chest for a split-second, he thought she was going to push him away.

A spark of panic raced through him. But he should have

known better than to assume anything when it came Maggie. Instead, she grabbed onto his shirt and pulled him closer to her. Molding his body against hers.

Fuck yes!

Taking that as his sign to proceed, he started pushing them toward her bed. He kissed her everywhere he could. Her lips, cheeks, jaw, anywhere he could reach. When he began kissing down her neck he felt the back of her legs hit the bed.

Thank fuck.

Trevor instantly pushed Maggie onto the bed, quickly following suit straddling her hips with his knees. "Goddamn," he growled before seeking out her mouth with his own.

He couldn't get enough of her. And at this moment he never wanted to.

Trevor wanted to fist pump the air when he was rewarded with Maggie opening her mouth as her tongue shot out, exploring his. He *knew* his girl would be just as feisty in bed as she was when she was verbally kicking his ass.

Trevor pulled away from her mouth when he felt her nails dig into his back as a new wave of pleasure shot through him. *Fuck yes! But wait until my shirt's off to mark me, baby. Mark me and mark me good.*

That thought nearly knocked the wind out of Trevor. He *never* let any of his partners mark him. Not even a hickey.

He couldn't help it though, there was just something about Maggie. He wanted her to mark him where everyone would see it.

Fuck he needed more. He looked down into her eyes, but what he saw staring back at him was as good as a cold bucket of water being thrown over him.

"Maggie?" he asked softly, trying to understand the terrified look in her eyes.

"I haven't done—"

"Shit! You're a virgin?" Half sickened half amazed, he

pulled back. How was anyone still a virgin at her age? At least he understood where that look was coming from now.

"No, you idiot!" She slapped him on the shoulder. "It's just... well... you know... I haven't done this a whole lot," she explained, worrying her bottom lip.

Trevor instantly relaxed. Then out of nowhere, something revved up inside of him. The thought of her being inexperienced set a new fire in him. The thought of another man seeing her, touching her curves, kissing her, made him want to break something.

A strange wave of possessiveness shot through Trevor as he leaned down, covering her body with his. Gazing into her eyes he softened his expression. With her being inexperienced, he didn't want to scare her off with his dominance.

"You're in charge," he assured her. "I do something you don't like, you let me know right away and I'll stop." He waited for her nod of acceptance before he placed his lips on hers again.

Fuck! She felt so good with her body cradled against his own, cushioning all his hard planes.

As Trevor pulled back from her lips he sat up still straddling her hips. He couldn't wait anymore. He looked down at her dress and made the split-second decision. "Off," he growled. He took hold of her dress and ripped it apart, right down the middle. The material easily split, baring her heavy breasts and rounded stomach to him.

His insides roared with the sight of her naked under him.

"You Neanderthal!" Maggie cried as she hurried to hide her stomach from him.

Oh, hell no! He'd been dreaming of her body for weeks now. No way in hell was she going to deny him that view. He grabbed both of her hands quickly pinning them above her head.

"Don't hide from me."

"You ripped my dress, you jackass!"

Trevor looked at the destroyed material. "Yep," he agreed. "I did and I'd do it again." Moving so he could pin both of her arms with one of his hands he pulled slightly away from her body. He gazed down at her. Her breasts were pert, her nipples standing at attention. The light pink coloring beckoned him to taste.

He shrugged. He wasn't going to deny himself. Not now, not ever. He leaned over, taking her right nipple into his mouth.

"Oh, God," Maggie moaned.

Oh, he wanted to hear more of that. He increased his suction causing her to let out another moan. "Dear God."

"Trevor will do." He laughed from around his treat. Ignoring her glare, he went back to his task. He sucked hard, letting her taste hit his senses. He wanted more of her. He wanted fucking all of her. After another second, he released her peak with a wet pop.

Trevor immediately kissed down her body. Her belly amazed him. Where he was used to hard bones protruding out, here he found a rounded cloud and softness. Hips that he could hold onto for days as he pounded into her. It was an eye-opening experience for him.

To have someone under him who cushioned him like no one had before, sent shivers down his spine. He didn't think he'd ever been harder than he was at this moment.

Trevor quickly let go of her pinned hands and ripped the rest of the dress in two. This left Maggie laying before him in nothing but black-lace panties.

Trevor couldn't have stifled his groan even if he wanted to. He reached for the material with one goal in mind. "Hips up," he got out through clenched teeth.

And to his surprise Maggie actually obeyed him. *That was*

a first. He didn't have time to bask in the victory, though. No, right now he was on a mission. A mission that a nuclear war wasn't going to stop him from.

"Holy fucking shit!" He gazed down at her once she was completely naked. His fingers lightly brushed against her swollen lower lips. "You're fucking bare," he growled deep in the back of his throat as he memorized her lush pussy in his mind.

Seeing her pink lips swollen with need, glistening with her juices almost had him shooting his load right then and there.

"Thank Lexi for that," Maggie moaned as his fingers danced along her opening.

"What?"

"She's an evil woman. My poor clit will never recover."

"I don't care what she is," he remarked. "She's my new fucking hero." His fingers brushed against Maggie's clit causing her hips to jump off the bed. "I think your clit's just fine." He chuckled sending her a wink.

"Shove it."

Ignoring her, he bent down licking her core from top to bottom.

"Mmm," a moan escaped her lips.

Trevor had to fight his own body for control as her taste erupted against his tongue. *How in the hell did she taste like fucking honey? That's not possible.*

He'd tasted many women in his day, and not one of them tasted anything even close to this.

Instantly, something snapped inside of him as he pulled away. "Next time will be better, I promise. Right now. Right fucking now I *need* to be inside of you."

129

NEXT TIME?

There wasn't going to be a next time.

No friggin' way. Over her dead body would this ever happen again. Just as Maggie was about to tell him that, he jumped from between her legs and disrobed faster than she'd ever thought possible.

The moment he pushed his pants down, her eyes widened.

Holy Crapolie!

Trevor was huge. How the hell had she missed that the day she walked in on him? Hell, how had she missed that ever? There were tons of movies he had to wear tight pants in.

She watched transfixed as his dick bounced from his movements. The head already glistening with need. Oh man, he was thick, really thick. How the hell was he even going to fit?

Nope, not gonna happen. She was about to close her legs when she watched him reach into his pants and pull out a condom. After rolling it on, he crawled back onto the bed and seated himself between her legs.

"I promise next time it'll be better. I *have* to be inside of you right now."

With that, Trevor spread her legs and in one swift movement plunged into her. At first, Maggie wanted to cringe, as she'd felt fuller than she'd ever had in her life.

"Fuck, you're so tight," Trevor growled as he leaned over her body, bringing his lips to hers. "You'll stretch, give it a second, baby. Hold on."

She nodded not trusting her words, as he filled her.

"God, baby, you're fuckin' perfect."

She wasn't, but this was not the time to argue.

Trevor's body shook as he ever so slowly pulled himself out of her center. He was almost completely out, just leaving the tip inside before he pushed back in.

"Oh God," she couldn't help but moan as the feeling took over her body.

Trevor began moving fast as he finally hit that spot deep inside of her that caused Maggie to scream out in pleasure.

"That's it, that's your spot, baby. Fuck yeah." He started moving faster, hitting her spot with every thrust.

"I'm gonna... oh shit... oh no..."

Trevor reached between them pinching her clit, as he moved his hips. The instant sensation caused stars to explode behind Maggie's eyes. Her whole body shook. "Trevor!"

He thrust faster and harder as she screamed out his name. "Yes, baby, yes!" He pushed one more time before spilling deep inside of her.

After emptying himself Trevor collapsed on to his side next to her on the bed. Rolling away from Maggie she saw Trevor dispose of the condom. When he was done he rolled back onto his side, moving to kiss her neck.

Maggie blinked as she tried to get her sense back. What in the fuck did she just do?

Trevor let out a moan as he leaned into her grinding his dick against her hip.

How was he still hard? Fuck, she still couldn't breathe right yet, how was he ready for round two?

Round two?

Maggie internally groaned. There should have never even been a round one.

What the hell am I doing? Maggie moved away from him, her body instantly protested, clearly feeling the loss of him. She placed one of her hands on her chest trying to control her erratic heartbeat.

This was Trevor McCain, the bane of her existence. This should *not* have happened. It was a hard and fast rule written in the "Don't Do Anything Stupid" book.

Struggling to catch her breath, she looked over at Trevor. She'd never seen him like this before. His face was hard, but not in the *I hate you* way it normally was. No, this was the, *I'm going to fuck you so hard, you won't be able to walk for a week* way.

She wanted to slap herself when a shiver ran through her body.

No, bad, Mags. Bad! She scolded herself.

Trevor hollered as he jumped. "What the fuck!"

Maggie afraid of what was going on quickly turned to face him.

"What the fuck is wrong with that thing?"

That's when Maggie looked at the end of the bed. Pocket decided to grace them with his presence. And, from the way he was staring at Trevor's feet, she could only surmise that Pocket decided Trevor's toes were the enemy and he needed to save them all from them.

"Pocket!" she scolded, but secretly she gave the cat a mental high five. Not only did he attack Trevor, but he also defused what could have been a very awkward situation.

"What the hell is *it* doing?" Trevor asked, staring at her cat like it was from a different planet.

"He's saving me," she replied.

"Holy fuck. Stop staring at my dick like that," he growled, trying to push the cat off the bed with his foot. If she was being honest, Pocket did look like his dick was the next Antichrist and he was sent to kill it.

Trevor pushed Pocket with his foot again. That's exactly what Pocket wanted to happen. He pounced on Trevor's foot, kicking and biting the only way Pocket knew how.

"That's it!" Trevor jumped and grabbed Pocket. "I swear to everything you're some kind of fucking alien creature." He moved to her bedroom door, Pocket now attacking his hands and arms like he was vanquishing a demon.

Stifling her laugh, she watched as Trevor carefully, well as carefully as he could, put Pocket out of the room closing the door so he couldn't come back in.

When Trevor turned to face her, his expression nearly knocked the wind out of her. Pure lust was staring back at her. Even after her cat tried to exorcise the demon out of him.

"Maggie." He took a step closer to her.

"Trevor, stay right there." Nope, this wasn't happening. Maggie pulled the covers over her body as the gravity of the situation started to sink in. *Holy shit!* Holy freaking shit.

To his credit, though, Trevor stopped his advance. She'd be lying if she said a pang of disappointment didn't run through her. She wanted him to stop. Well, at least she thought she did.

"I want you again," he purred like a rare honey poured from his lips as he spoke.

Maggie couldn't help but look at him dumbfounded. "Umm?"

"No," he growled. "I *need* you." He took one step closer to her. "You're a fucking pain in my ass. You're loud, blunt, and annoying, but all I want to do is to fuck you from here until next week. I want to feel your curves around me. Listen as you scream my name over and over again until you lose your voice."

Maggie swallowed hard as she shook her head. "Nope. You've lost your mind and you're delusional."

Trevor moved his hand to his crotch, pumping it up and down a few times. "Do you think this lies?"

Maggie didn't quite know how to respond. She watched as he pumped himself, staring her down like he was a starving man and she was his only meal. If she wasn't already laying on the bed, her knees would have given out.

Wait. No. This has to stop. This was wrong.

This was Trevor McCain, *the* Trevor McCain, standing in front of her, wanting her, no, *needing* her as he liked to put it. But that wasn't it. This was the man that got his jollies off by messing with her life, humiliating her in front of everyone.

The same man that not only an hour ago told her she was screwing some guy on the dance floor.

No. She was better than this. Maggie was way better than this... So what the hell had she just done?

Chapter Sixteen

MAGGIE WATCHED as Trevor crawled over the bed to her. Her heart raced as she felt her body react to him. *Bad body, very bad!*

Maggie looked toward the door and then back at him. As if Pocket understood her need, she heard her cat run, what she assumed was full speed at her bedroom door trying to break in, causing a loud thud.

Don't worry baby, as soon as I can get out of this mess I'll buy you a steak. Oh, and take the hinges off the door.

"Maggie," Trevor distracted her from her thoughts as he reached for her.

No! No, no, no.

Maggie quickly jumped from the bed, trying to pull the blanket with her. Unfortunately for her, she didn't account for Trevor's massive weight to counteract her pull. Before she knew it, she was falling to the floor.

"Owwie." Her ass hit the ground.

Trevor quickly moved to the side of the bed. "Shit, Maggie, are you okay?" He reached for her but she jerked herself away from him.

"No," she answered.

"What?" Not really questioning Maggie he once again reached for her. "Is your ass okay?"

She turned her head to glare at him.

"What?" His brows shot up in surprise as he smirked. She hated that smug smirk, but not as much as she hated him right now. "It's a mighty fine ass you have there, Maggie. I don't want anything to happen to it."

Did he think this was a joke?

"Come here, baby." Trevor reached for the blanket trying to pull it away from her grasp. Which only caused her to yank the blanket more securely around her as she tried with all her might to kick at him.

"Back away," she growled.

Trevor held his hands up in surrender. "Whoa."

"Don't whoa me, Trevor. You need to leave and leave now." She pointed toward the bedroom door. The faster she got him out of there, the faster she could figure out a way to fix this mess.

Trevor stared down at her, his eyes hardening.

Why the hell was he mad at her now? This was all a total mess.

She glared back at him and to her horror, she soon realized her eyes slowly drifted down his body. His very naked body. The naked body that she had just gotten very acquainted with.

Oh God, oh God, oh God, it jumped like it was mocking her.

"Maggie."

She shot her eyes to Trevor's face. When she saw his smirk her first reaction was to jump up and smack it off. Leave it to him to cause her mind to lose all common sense. "Trevor, you need to leave."

"No," he answered. "What we need to do is talk and after we talk, I'm going to bend you over the side of the bed." He pointed to the spot she just fell from. "Right there and fuck you. *Hard.*"

Who in the hell did this man think he was? Did he think because he was showing her some sort of attention, she would follow him blindly to whatever he wanted? Hell no! Trevor fucking McCain caused her more grief than she thought was possible in only a few short weeks.

Hell, freaking no!

Maggie shook with anger. He was treating her the same way her mother used to. Maggie was supposed to jump for joy whenever her mother showed her an ounce of kindness. And, if she were being honest with herself, there were more times than she could count where she would do whatever her mother would want in hopes her mother would say she was proud of her, or even that she loved her.

No, she was *never* falling back into that pattern again.

And, here was Trevor pretty much doing the exact same thing her mother did. What, because he showed a fatty some attention, she needed to bow down to him?

Fuck that!

"Trevor," she growled while getting to her feet. She was careful to keep the blanket around her. No need to add to the biggest mistake of her life by showing him the goods, once again. "You need to leave right now."

"I'm not leaving," he stated matter-of-fact.

"Yes." Maggie moved to the door and opened it. "You are."

TREVOR WATCHED as Pocket ran full speed into the bedroom with one goal in mind. The second he saw the creature lock eyes with his dangly appendage he did his best to shield himself.

"What the fuck?" he cried, trying to push away the cat that was eyeing him in a way that made his skin crawl.

"You need to leave," Maggie repeated.

Trevor looked at Maggie who was standing at the door not looking at him. Her posture said it all, though. She was conflicted, and the truth was he understood why. How could he not? He was a fucking asshole to her, and instead of, he didn't know, just being nice, he let his dick do the talking instead of actually using his words.

None had ever gotten to him like Maggie did and now... well now... *Fuck! I screwed this up.*

Looking down at Pocket, the cat blinked slowly at him, then his eyes locked on where his hand was covering his goods.

Damn it. He never went this far for anyone. Hell, normally when he was done screwing someone, the first thing he did was bolt. Not here, though.

It was like Maggie was pulling him in at every turn. Even now as he looked at her. Her cheeks were red, her hair all over the place, her arms tightly holding up that stupid blanket, blocking the view he desperately wanted.

Fuck, she was beautiful.

He blanched at himself. *Beautiful?* He never called anyone beautiful. Sure, chicks were hot, or fuckable, but no, this was... oh man, he could stare at her all day and never get enough.

When he didn't move, Maggie *finally* looked his way. It pissed him off she refused to look into his eyes though.

"Trevor, this was a mistake. A huge fucking mistake. I know we've never gotten along and that you love making my life hell, but just this once can you please just get dressed and get the hell out."

Making her life hell?

Trevor gaped at her. "Making your life hell? I don't make your life hell." He cocked his brow at her.

Maggie's expression instantly changed from conflict and

despair to all-out war within seconds. "Are you kidding me?"

"No." Trevor crossed his arms over his chest not caring about protecting his manhood anymore. "I have never made your life hell. Name one instance where I made your life hell. If I remember correctly, which I do, I've done nothing to ever cause you anything but—"

"Oh my God, you *are* actually fucking crazy. A certifiable crazy person!" She stomped away from the door and toward him. "I can name more than one instance where you went out of your way to make my life hell. How about the first friggin' time we met? You tried to get me fired, or how about when I was at the coffee shop with Lexi and Danny? Hmm... Oh yeah, and what about the fucking shit you pulled at your house? You practically called me a slut and insisted that it was my fault that some waiter fell on me... and what if I bring up all the goddamn uncalled shit you've said!"

Pocket bellowed agreeing with her.

Ignoring the screeching, Trevor looked into the eyes of this feisty, hellcat standing before him. His dick instantly hardened. The fire in her eyes caused sparks to shoot through his body. He was not going to back down from this, or her. Not now. Not when for the first time in his life there was a person that ignited everything inside of him.

"If I recall," he started, trying to use his size to intimidate her, which he knew would only get her to go toe to toe with him again. "You didn't get fired, I took you home when your car crapped out, oh and fucking paid for the repairs. All of them. And bought you this for your fucking birthday." He reached past her, grabbed his pants pulling out the necklace. "But you refuse to even acknowledge it. Not only that, you left it at my house like the ungrateful pain in my ass you are!"

Trevor shoved the necklace in her hands.

Why in the hell was she always like this? Didn't she understand he was trying to make it better?

Maggie held the necklace tightly in her grasp as her eyes narrowed fully at him. "You have got to be the most self-centered, egotistical, pain in my fucking ass I have ever come in contact with. I think you have officially surpassed my mother."

Why couldn't she just understand all the good I've done for her? Her car repairs were not cheap. And, in all of his existence on earth, unless it was his family he had never *ever* bought anyone a gift. *Didn't she understand that?*

Fuck this. She was driving him insane. Post sex was supposed to feel great. Instead, all he wanted to do was strangle her and tie her to the bed and fuck her again. He needed to get out of there before he told her. "You know what? You're right." He pulled on his pants. "I'm outta here."

"Thank the Universe."

Trevor narrowed his eyes dangerously at her as he walked out of her bedroom door, her cat following right behind him. If it wasn't bad enough she was a royal pain in his ass, her cat seemed to have it out for him too. Ignoring the ambush attacks on his ankles he made it to her front door. After opening it he looked over his shoulder.

Maggie stood there, the blanket tightly wrapped around her accentuating her curves. Curves that he'd now had the pleasure of exploring. Curves he knew he would be exploring again soon. "This isn't over."

With that, he walked through her door slamming it behind him. He waited a few seconds until he heard the tell-tale sign of the lock clicking into place.

Trevor let out a heavy sigh as he walked down the hallway a smile appearing on his face.

Nope, this was far from over.

Trevor's smile grew from ear to ear as he recalled the way Maggie clung onto the necklace like it was her only lifeline.

With an extra pep in his step, Trevor whistled as he made his way down to his SUV.

Chapter Seventeen

MAGGIE WALKED into Perk You Up the next morning groggy and sore. There was no surprise there. No matter how hard she tried, she wasn't able to get to sleep after Trevor stormed out.

Thoughts of him kept replaying in her mind over and over again. And, if it wasn't him, it was that stupid necklace.

Not to mention every move she'd make, her body screamed in protest reminding her of how stupid she'd been.

Subconsciously, Maggie reached into the front pocket of her jeans. Her fingertips grazed the jewelry that was safely tucked away. Her stupid body betrayed her with its sudden relaxation of knowing it was still safely on her. Maggie tried to walk out of her apartment leaving it behind. However, she was only able to make it a few feet before turning back to get it. Which ultimately annoyed her even more than she already was.

"Mags, love," Lexi chirped from behind the counter.

Jerked out of her thoughts, Maggie smiled at her friend. She knew coming to Perk You Up would fix all the craziness that was surrounding her. "Hi, Lex."

Lexi stared at her, her head cocked a little to the side making a purple ringlet fall out of place. Maggie took a deep breath hoping that Lexi was just doing her, "coffee magic" and not analyzing her thoughts.

A quick sharp nod accompanied by thin lips had Maggie's heart plummet. *Oh no.*

"I'll be over in a few with your drink, missy. *And,* as soon as the rush leaves, *I'll* be over." With that, Lexi turned from her to make whatever drink she'd decided was in order for Maggie. However, Maggie could tell something had changed in Lexi's demeanor. Her posture was stiff, and her foot tapped with annoyance.

Great just great. Maybe getting the taxi over here wasn't the best idea.

Doing her best to ignore what she knew was coming, Maggie moved to find a spot by the window. Yep, she was sure of it now. Coming here wasn't such a good idea.

A few minutes later, Lexi brought her over a mug. "Drink up, love. I'll be over in a little while and we will have ourselves a little chit-chat. No need to be upset over that jerk." Maggie physically relaxed. Lexi must have thought she was still upset at the way Trevor treated her at his house. *Whew, okay,* she could deal with that.

Maggie sat back bringing the mug up to her nose and inhaling deeply. Cinnamon and nutmeg. *Mmm.* She took a sip and her eyes nearly rolled back into her head. It was as if Christmas was poured into a mug. She closed her eyes taking another sip. Comfort washed over her. She was taken back to the holidays she would spend with her Grammie.

They were some of her best memories. Waking up on Christmas morning, Grammie greeting her with her special Christmas breakfast. Grammie never had much money, but she never let that hinder their holidays. She would fill Christmas with so much love and joy, Maggie never needed anything. Most of the time, Grammie just got her something really small and watched movies with her all day long.

To Maggie it was perfect.

Taking another sip, she opened her eyes in search of Lexi. She was behind the counter bouncing around as she filled orders and chatted with her regulars. How in the heck she knew that Maggie needed a "comfort" drink was beyond her. Shaking her head trying to figure out how she did it, she decided to leave well enough alone and admire the view from the window.

Absentmindedly, Maggie reached into her pocket and pulled out the necklace. It was beautiful, the diamond star was breathtaking.

Maggie let the pendant glide through her fingers as she examined the shine. In all her life, she'd never received a gift like this. It was by far the most expensive, beautiful item she'd ever had the pleasure of holding in her hands.

She bunched the necklace in her grasp as she shut her eyes tightly. She felt like an idiot. Grammie would be so disappointed in her.

"Wha' cha got there, hun?"

Maggie opened her eyes to see Lexi sitting across from her. A mug in her hands as she took a sip. "Uh, nothing," she answered.

"Uh-huh," Lexi remarked. "That the necklace?"

Giving up the charade, Maggie opened her hand to reveal the pendant. She still didn't know why she brought it with her or why she kept touching it.

"It is beautiful," Lexie remarked. "I'm actually kinda surprised you still have it. I thought you said you threw it back at him at his house."

Maggie looked at the pendant. "I did."

"Okay." Lexi cocked her head to the side.

"After you guys dropped me back home Trevor showed up."

Lexi sat her drink down and moved to the edge of her seat, her face going hard and her lips tightened. "Did something happen? I thought you were just upset about the way he treated you at his place. I swear to God if he did anything else to upset you I will beat the shit out of him *and* start putting laxatives in his coffee."

For the first time since everything happened, Maggie threw her head back and laughed. Leave it to Lexi to not only go to the extreme but to find a way to really hit the person where it hurt. "Well, I mean, I'm not going to stop you if it's your lifelong mission to make him suffer." She laughed as she wiped a tear from her eye.

"I'd do it just for you, babe." Lexi's face lit as she picked up her drink and took a sip. Her eyes showing all the mischief possible in one person. Over her cup, she said, "For reals though, hun, what happened after he showed up?"

Maggie coming back to the realization that last night really did happen and she needed someone to talk to, closed her eyes and took a pained breath. "I don't even know where to start."

"Normally the beginning."

Maggie rolled her eyes. "Yeah, well... Shit, Lexi. I screwed up. I've made a mess out of this."

"I'm sure you didn't, Mags, and even if someone did mess up, I am one hundred percent positive that it was Trevor's fault. Didn't we decide it was always going to be his fault?"

Maggie blew out a breath. If only it were that easy. "I was in my room trying to get out of that skin-tight dress... alone." She glared at Lexi who shrugged. "And, out of nowhere, he was there, in my room."

"He broke in?" Lexi panicked and then threw her drink on the table. "Let me at him!"

"Simmer down, killer." Maggie threw her hands up.

Lexi glared at her but sat back down, motioning for her to go on.

"Anyway, I guess I didn't lock my door and after not getting a response from me when he knocked, he checked the knob and was able to get in. God Lexi, I was dancing around with my arms flailing everywhere trying to get out of that damn dress." She groaned.

"Yeah, those dresses are made for someone else to get you out of them."

"I know that now." Maggie glared at her. "Anyway, we started arguing and it got pretty heated. We were toe to toe when..." she trailed off.

"When what? When what? I swear to God woman I will murder you where you sit. Do not keep me waiting." Lexi moved to the edge of her seat.

Looking down, Maggie rushed out, "Weslepttogether."

"Excuse me?"

Maggie refused to look at her.

"Repeat what you said, Maggie."

"We had a fight," she said, finally looking at her. Lexi's eyes were wide and her body was stiff.

"No, ma'am after the fight. You and Trevor what?"

"We uh, sorta, you know."

"No, I don't know."

"We slept together, banged, bumped uglies, you know, did *it.*"

Lexi sat there staring at Maggie as if she'd grown another head. She was about to make sure Lexi was still breathing when a smile spread across her face. She jumped from her seat and started doing a happy dance.

"What are you doing?" Maggie asked trying to get Lexi to sit back down.

"Yay! Yay! Yay!"

"Lexi, sit down. Now!"

"Hell no! You got yourself some! And, from Trevor, mmhhmmm what a fine man he is! Yay! Total asshole and we still hate him for how he treated you but you won. You brought him down to his knees. Didn't I tell you curves are what drive men wild?" She did another spin.

"Lexi, this is not a celebration. It was a mistake a *huge* mistake and now I need your help to figure out what to do next."

Lexi sat back down not even trying to hide her enthusiasm. "What do you mean mistake?"

"Lexi, I hate the guy."

"There is a fine line between love and hate," she mumbled while taking another sip of her drink smiling even wider.

"I'm being serious here."

"So am I. All right, so you slept with him. Is he good? Did he make you scream?"

"*Lexi!*"

"What? I've been dying to know if all the rumors are true."

"Can we please be serious here and find a way for me to fix my completely fucked up life?"

Lexi put her drink down. "I don't know why you think this is such a bad thing? He obviously likes you. He took you home that day, fixed your car without you knowing... I need to thank him for that," she said, looking away. "No laxative in the first coffee I give him. All the others are still up for debate. If he likes you then he sure as hell needs to find another way to tell you rather than some *playground bully the girl you like cause you don't know how to use your words shit*." She looked back at Maggie. "But anyway, he's been good to you. Plus, he bought you that beautiful necklace you have *yet* to let go of."

Maggie dropped the necklace onto the table as if she'd just been burned by it. Lexi went to grab it but Maggie snatched it back up involuntarily. *Shit!*

"It obviously means a lot to you. Tell me, Mags, what's so bad about what happened between you two?"

"Are you kidding me? He's a jerk."

"Yeah, most men are."

"Danny's not." There was a wistful look that ran across Lexi's face.

Lexi cleared her throat. "We are not talking about Danny, Maggie. We are talking about you and Trevor. What is so bad about him that you can't enjoy yourself?"

"He's a rude, pompous asshole. He made my life a living hell and you know that firsthand. Not to mention all the mean things he's said about me. *To my face,*" Maggie growled.

Lexi sat back in her chair and nodded. "I will give you that. Trevor can be an ass, and he *was* an ass to you. Hence, the reason I have decided to add the extra ingredient in his coffee, but and I mean this, he only did that when he first met you. As time has gone by, he's actually started changing his ways around you." She held up her hand. "And, I know being nice now is absolutely no excuse for the things he's said to you and about you in the past. If it were me, I would make him apologize every single day for a year between my legs, and only after that year was up, I would decide if he were worthy enough but—"

"Jesus, Lexi!"

"What? You wanted honesty here and I am giving it to you. Is Trevor an asshole for saying those things and acting the way he did? Yes. But do I think you should forgive him and see where this could go? Yes. And, you want to know why, Maggie Connolly? It's because you deserve to be happy for once in your life. You deserve to be able to wake up each morning and not question if you are good enough in a world full of hateful jerkwad people. And, I think Trevor can do that for you. Even if it just for fun for a little while. Get yourself laid and laid often and once you've gotten your fill, decide what to do then.

Hell, keep him and let him fuck your brains out every day. That's what I would do."

Maggie sat there completely dumbfounded. This was Lexi, her *best* friend, and she was evidently on Trevor's side here. No. Lexi needed to be on her side. The side where she hated Trevor and thought he was a jerk and was going to spend the next few hours trying to come up with a plan to fix the mistake Maggie made. Not trying to put her together with Trevor. Maggie narrowed her eyes. "How do you know this wasn't one of his famous one-night stands? Huh? How do you know he's not out there talking crap about me right now?"

Strangely Lexi smiled at Maggie before picking up her drink and standing she nodded to the necklace. "That's how I know this isn't a one-night stand type of thing. Do I agree with a lot that Trevor's done and said? No. But, I've known him since the first day I opened this place. Deep down he is a good guy. He's got a lot of walls up around him just like *you.* He's been hurt in the past and that man doesn't know who to trust or who is really his friend to save his life. But beneath all of that, he's just as vulnerable as you are. Giving you that necklace meant something to him. He wouldn't have done that if he was just trying to get into your pants."

Maggie sat back in the chair with her mouth open.

"And, I know for a fact, he isn't out there talking shit about you right now," she said before walking away.

"How do you know that?" Maggie asked.

Looking over her shoulder she motioned to the door. "He's walking in the door right now."

Chapter Eighteen

TREVOR SMILED as he opened the door to Perk You Up. He hadn't felt this good for as long as he could remember. Every time he closed his eyes, he would see Maggie laying naked underneath him. Her hair sprawled out on the pillows, her face red.

Maggie was a sight he would never forget.

Instantly, his body respond. *Down boy! We gotta wait.*

When he walked through the door the first thing Trevor saw was Lexi behind the counter. Her smile wider than it normally was. Why was she always so happy in the mornings? *Annoying.* He rolled his eyes, but let it be. Everyone deserved to be happy. And he wasn't going to let her rain on his parade.

Trevor then saw Lexi's eyes flick toward the window.

That's when he saw her.

Maggie was staring at him, her eyes wide and her face pale.

Trevor couldn't help the smile that came over him. Instead of going toward the counter he turned and headed straight toward Maggie. He caught the shine from the necklace in her hands. His heart skipped a beat and his smile grew wider as he quickened his pace.

When he reached her, he opened his mouth to say hello, but she shot up and pushed past him instead. "Maggie, wait!" he hollered as she ran out the door. He went to follow her only to have a hand pull him back.

"Let her go," Lexi said while handing him a drink. "This time you're lucky, mister."

Her eyes shot to his drink. *Did she do something to it?* Why in the world was she so weird? "Why am I lucky?"

"Oh, nothing," she answered in her singsong voice. "Tomorrow, when you try your coffee keep in mind, I am trying out some new recipes. It might taste a little different."

"Uh, okay." He turned to head out of the door in search of Maggie.

"Let her go," she repeated. "At least for right now. She's had a rough morning."

Dread shot through him. Had she gone to Lexi and told her what happened? Had he hurt her? His morning was beyond perfect, but now knowing Maggie was upset made him want to punch something. "What happened?"

Lexi gave him the *look*.

Okay, so she knew...

"How about we have a little chat..." She motioned to the seat Maggie had vacated.

Trevor looked at the door and back to the seat. Everything inside of him wanted to go after Maggie, but he also knew that it was better to have this conversation with Lexi now rather than later. Sighing he walked to the seat, Lexi following behind him. "Let's cut the crap."

"Yes, let's cut the crap. You like Maggie and have feelings for her."

"No, it's just—"

She cut him off with a look.

"Okay," he stated.

"I'm not here to mess around, Trevor. We are here to have a serious conversation."

He looked at her. Could he admit to her he had feelings for Maggie? It's not like he really had strong feelings for her. She was—Nope. He couldn't deny it. He definitely had feelings for her. Huge feelings, ones that he didn't see going away anytime soon.

Trevor cleared his throat. "Clearly, you already know what happened last night. And, before you say anything I am not apologizing for any of it. Okay, well maybe the way I acted could have been questionable and... Actually no, I was a gentleman the whole time. Whatever she told you was a lie."

"I see," Lexi said. "So, you did break into her house and ravish her?"

"I didn't break in, she left the door unlocked!" he growled.

"Uh-huh."

"She did and I didn't break in. I went to give her back the necklace she left and just talk. I knocked, but she didn't answer. I tried the knob and it opened. When I walked in she looked like she was being electrocuted."

Lexi laughed. "She is interesting."

Trevor barked out a laugh. It felt good to laugh. "Yeah. Regardless though, one thing led to another and before I knew it, we were naked playing a game of Twister."

"Twister." She laughed. "Maggie didn't quite put it that way."

"She was probably being modest."

Lexi's eyes beamed. "Sure."

"Lexi, I don't know what she said to you, but—"

"Trevor," she cut him off. "I've known you for a long time. A *very* long time. I've gotten to know you over the years. The moment you took her home because of her car, I knew something started to change in you. Paying for her piece of crap car, by the way, thank you for that, even if she hasn't said thank you yet. I want to thank you."

Trevor nodded.

"What solidified your change for me was the necklace. You don't do that, Trevor. Although, you have made some shitty choices in a lot of places in your life, doing all of this just to sleep with her is not one of them."

"It's not just about sleeping with her," he growled, his features hard. He hated being this exposed. More than that, he hated how Lexi could take one look at a person and know everything there was about them.

"I know." She reached out and grabbed his hand. "Trevor, you have to understand. Sure, you changed. You want to be with her. But—"

"What?" he asked. Was she going to tell him to leave Maggie alone? He didn't think he could do that even if he tried at this point. She was all he thought about.

Taking a deep breath, she started, "I don't know the whole story, but it wasn't good where she came from. Even her mother wasn't the best to her. Constantly picking on her every chance she got. All Maggie really had was her grandmother. Her mother..."

Lexi's eyes showed so much anger it almost made Trevor recoil.

"She's a complete waste of a mother if you ask me. And you..." She poked him in the chest. "You said some of the same things her mother has said to her. So, you need to understand it's going to take a lot to get her to let her walls down. And for you, those walls are ten times higher. Sure, she let you have her body at a moment of weakness, but the damage you have already done to her will take a lot to repair."

Shit!

Trevor knew the things he had said about her were dick moves. He knew that he was going to have to fight like hell to get her to understand he was serious. But, hearing about her own mother treating her like shit pissed him off.

She'd mentioned something about her mother when they were fighting in the house, but he hadn't thought much of it. Now, he wished he would have asked her about it. Anger rose through him. What kind of mother picks on their own kid? He didn't know what he would do without his mother. When he first told her he wanted to be an actor, she was over the moon for him. She was his biggest and best support system.

"You've got your work cut out for you," she said. "But I think she's worth it. You need someone like her, Trevor. You need someone you can trust, someone *you* can let your walls down around. You need to have someone that you *know* isn't using you because you're famous and have tons of money."

"No one uses me."

She gave him that look again. *How in the hell did she do that?*

"I'm serious here, Trevor. I would be the first one to drop-kick your ass if I thought you would hurt her, but I honestly think she is exactly what you need."

He didn't know what to say so he stared at her. He watched as she put her hand on his arm and squeezed lightly. "And, Trevor, you have and will always have friends and people you can trust." She pointed to herself. "You do have true friends. I'm one of them, and if you stop being an asshole to Danny, I know he would be one too."

With those parting words, she left.

Trevor stared at her for a moment before he decided that she was right. He grabbed his drink and headed for the door. Maggie was worth it. No matter the stories he told himself in the beginning, and the uphill battle he knew he'd have. There was something about Maggie that made her worth it and it was time he stopped pussyfooting around it.

He had feelings for Maggie.

Huge feelings.

TREVOR PACED AROUND his living room. He still couldn't believe he'd done it. What was he thinking? He could have figured this out on his own he didn't need to—

His doorbell rang interrupting his thought.

"Shit."

Trevor walked to the door and opened it. "Hey man, thanks for coming over." He watched as Danny gave him a once-over.

"Sure," Danny answered. "You sounded kinda desperate."

Trevor groaned. He *was* desperate. "Yeah, well," he mumbled. "Come in and make yourself at home."

Danny walked past him and into the living room.

"Can I get you anything?"

"Tell me why I am here, Trevor," Danny demanded.

Clearing his throat, Trevor quickly glanced around the room before looking at Danny. "Yeah, okay. Sure." He crossed his arms over his chest. "Here's the thing. Other than Lexi, you are Maggie's best friend and I need your help."

Danny narrowed his eyes at him. "Why?"

Trevor couldn't blame the guy for being cautious. He might as well bite the bullet. "I like her, okay. And not like some stupid Hollywood fling. I actually want to get to know her better." There he said it. "I mean, I really like her, and I've screwed up a lot. I need to make this right. I thought we were on the right path after last night. I mean why would she sleep with me if she still pretty much—" Trevor didn't see it coming.

"You did what?!" The impact of Danny's fist on his jaw hurt like hell.

"Shit!" Any other time he would have swung back, but he

had to give this to Danny. If the roles were reversed, he would have done the same thing.

"You fucking asshole." Danny went to hit him again, but Trevor stopped him.

"Slow your roll, man."

"Slow my roll? What the hell is wrong with you?"

"Okay, I get it. You want to beat the shit out of me right now, and well, I don't really blame you but listen to me. It's not what you are thinking, I didn't force her or anything like that. It just happened."

"So, your dick just so happened to land inside of her?"

"No," he corrected, shaking his head. "Calm down a second, Rambo. I didn't ask you here so you could *try* and kick my ass, 'cause we all know I would win that fight. I asked you here to help me win her over. I want to be with her. Fuck, Danny, I have never wanted someone so bad in my life. I fucking eat, sleep, and breathe her. And, yeah, I'll admit it, normally after I fuck someone, I never think of them again, but Maggie is different. I don't think I can ever get enough of her. Not in this lifetime or the next."

Trevor sat down, completely defeated. If this was what relationships were about, he wanted nothing to do with them. He hung his head in his hands trying to make the rampant feelings subside. How in the hell had one chick with extra curves come in and turned his whole world upside down?

He felt the cushion next to his sink down.

"You know," Trevor continued, his head still in his hands. "I didn't know it at first, but I was jealous of you. I am *never* jealous." He looked at Danny. "The thought of you being with her nearly tore me in two. That's why I was such a prick. At least partly."

"You were a prick," Danny agreed.

"Yeah, I know. I don't even know how it happened. One

moment I was doing fine, living my life the way I'd always lived it, and then out of nowhere she was under my skin."

Danny sighed. "I know exactly how you feel."

That took Trevor by surprise. Did Danny love Maggie? The new unfamiliar spark of possessiveness ran through him as he growled causing Danny to hold up his hands in surrender.

"Not Maggie. Yeah, I love Maggie as a best friend and sister, but not like that. I'm just saying I know how you feel about going on with your life and then the next moment someone is there turning your world into a crazy mess and you don't know which end is up."

Trevor watched him, his head cocked to the side... *that's interesting. Who could he be talking about?*

Neither one of them spoke for a while. The silence was only broken when Danny looked at Trevor. "You really like her, don't you? This isn't just a fling for you, is it?"

Without missing a beat Trevor answered. "No. This isn't a fling for me. Trust me I know I've fucked up here and honestly she'd have every right to kick me to the curb and never speak to me again but I... there is something about her I crave when she's not around."

After a few minutes of Danny staring him down, he nodded. "Okay. I have some ideas."

For the next three hours, Danny and Trevor worked out some promising ideas he could implement to win Maggie's heart. The whole time Trevor kept hinting at things Danny could do to win his mystery girl's heart too. Although, he didn't think it was much of a mystery as their night went on.

By the time Danny left, Trevor was pleased with their progress. And even though he hated that Lexi was right, he could see Danny being a good friend to him.

Ignoring the foreign feeling, Trevor pulled out his phone to find the nearest pet store. He needed some cat toys.

Chapter Nineteen

MAGGIE PACED AROUND her living room trying to wrap her head around everything going on in her life. Pocket was right on her tail swerving between her legs causing her to trip every few seconds.

"Pocket, can you knock it off? Can't you see your mommy is having an existential crisis?"

Pocket looked at her, a slow blink going across his eyes before opening his mouth and screeching louder than she'd ever heard.

"Pocket! For the love of all things sweet and delicious can you just not?"

Pocket strolled over to her then proceeded to attack her leg.

"Jesus!"

While Maggie was trying to dislodge her devil cat from her body, there was a knock on her door.

"Ugh," Maggie huffed. "This is the last thing I need." She walked to the door throwing it open. "What do you—"

"Did you even look to see who it was?" Trevor interrupted as he walked past her into the room.

You have got to be kidding me! She looked up at the ceiling. *I think you sit up there and purposely do things to make my life difficult.* She turned to Trevor. "What are you doing here?"

"Was your door even locked?" he asked, his brows pulled tightly together as he let out a small growl. Who in the hell gave him the right to barge into *her* home and then be pissed at *her*?

"Do not make me teach you a lesson," he warned.

Maggie's eyes widened, but she quickly recovered as she crossed her arms over her chest. "You've got two seconds to explain why you're here before I kick your ass."

"Kick my ass?" Trevor barked out a hearty laugh. "Please, please let me see you try and kick my ass. I'd pay money for it."

Maggie let out a growl before charging him.

Trevor effortlessly caught her mid-flight swinging her around in the air before they both ended up on the couch with Trevor pinning her under him. "Actually, this worked out really well." He gave her a cocky smile before leaning in to kiss her.

That bastard.

Unfortunately for her, he wasn't stupid enough to linger. After the quick peck, he jumped from the couch and covered his junk.

Maggie narrowed her eyes at him. The jerk knew exactly what she was going to do. She sat there on her couch glaring at him, not moving, causing Trevor to shrug and assume she was no longer going to go after him. *Stupid man.*

Right when she was about to go in for her attack, Trevor sat on the floor and reached for a bag that was not there a few minutes ago.

Maggie's eyes widened when she saw what Trevor pulled out.

"Pocket," Trevor called while putting the cat toy that looked like a mouse on the floor.

Pocket hearing his name appeared out of nowhere with a strategic dive bomb right onto Trevor's lap.

"Umph," Trevor groaned as he tried to maneuver the cat onto the floor. "The toy's down there, dumbass. *Not* on my lap."

True to Pocket's form, he opened his mouth and yelled, arguing with the man who was now pulling out more toys from the bag trying to entice Pocket to play with them instead of his appendages.

At first, Maggie stared at the two, like she'd entered into some warp reality. She was sure her mind was playing tricks on her. Was Trevor actually sitting on the floor playing with her cat? The cat he swore was *not* a cat.

And he bought Pocket toys? Toys, honest to God cat toys.

There is no way this was happening. No one and she meant no one had ever done anything like that for her.

Wait, she glared at him. *Was he trying to get Pocket on his side?* She questioned his antics for a moment, but the second Pocket dropped the tiny mouse and went for Trevor's forearm instead, she dismissed the idea. No one was stupid enough to try and lure the devil cat away from her. The cat had a mind of its own and it was tough even for her to try and tame him. She still couldn't get the hang of it. Lord knows she tried.

Maggie cautiously lowered herself to the floor, She wasn't really sure what was going on, but thinking about what Lexi said, she might as well see what happened. At least for this moment they weren't fighting for once. Maggie picked up the feather toy and within seconds Pocket was leaping from Trevor's arm and onto the feathers that were now flying around. Maggie couldn't help but laugh when she realized Pocket's purr was louder than she had ever heard.

"Oh, thank fuck." Trevor looked at his arm. "I didn't know how much longer my skin would have held out."

Maggie turned to stare at him as Pocket pranced around with the feathers.

"I'm glad Pocket liked it. I was worried he wouldn't have liked the feathers. You know they're not very manly." Trevor cleared his throat when she continued to stare at him. "Are you just gonna keep staring at me?"

"Did you really bring my cat toys?" she asked, not looking away from him.

"Yeah."

THIS WAS GOING MUCH BETTER than Trevor had anticipated.

This must be the first time in history that Maggie was actually *not* running her mouth. He wanted to laugh, but kept it in. She was just sitting there staring at him with her mouth open.

He fought the urge to lean over and kiss her. He knew he needed to chill, though, even the small peck from before had set him on fire.

What in the world were her lips made of?

Clearing his throat, Trevor picked up the mouse and started waving it around to get Pocket's attention.

"I don't even know what to say," Maggie finally spoke.

He wanted her to jump all over *him* with gratitude. Maybe rip off her shirt to show she was really thankful, but he knew that was a long shot. If the roles were reversed, which they never would be, that's what he would've done. Instead Trevor just shrugged.

He moved to pick up the cat which resulted in Pocket attacking his hand. At least he always knew how Pocket was always going to react. "I also brought us some movies we can watch. I remember seeing you had a DVD player. Old school. I like it. I normally just stream everything."

Maggie looked around the room nervously. "Uh, yeah. Something like that."

Trevor kind of liked catching her off guard and if you were to ask him, his plan was working perfectly. "Great. What do you want to watch, I've got some comedies and also some classic horror films?"

Maggie's face lit at the mention of horror films. *Thank you, Danny.* Trevor stood, giving Pocket a moving target now. "Where's your remote?"

Mindlessly, Maggie reached for the remote and handed it to him. As she did it, Trevor couldn't help the smile that spread across his face. Quickly he put in one of the horror films he brought. Once the movie stared, he moved back to her couch and sat next to her.

He'd be lying if he said he wasn't a little freaked out with her silence, but Trevor figured he'd just go with it for now.

About ten minutes into the movie he heard Maggie sigh. "This was a movie my Grammie and I used to watch all the time."

He nodded, not really sure what to say.

"I honestly can't wrap my head around you being here right now, or the fact that we're watching this movie."

"Well, I am here."

"I must be in *The Twilight Zone*," she whispered. "You know this exact movie was the one my grandma put on for me the first time my mother forgot to pick me up from school. Instead of walking home, I decided to walk to her house. Best decision I ever made in my life."

Trevor's heart sank. "How old were you?" When he looked her in the eyes there was a small trace of tears.

"I was seven."

Seven?

How could a mother forget their seven-year-old child? At seven he was constantly surrounded by his mother. She was always there for him, and never missed an opportunity to volunteer at his school.

"My Grammie was good at making me feel wanted and special. I was always welcome at her house no matter what time it was, day or night. She would open the door with her arms wide, ready to help me through anything."

"She sounds like a wonderful woman."

"She was. She was my rock." Maggie laughed sarcastically. "You know, she was the only one that didn't laugh in my face when I told her I wanted to be an actor."

Maggie focused on the TV. "I remember when I told my mom that's what I wanted to be. Instead of supporting me, she told me no one in Hollywood would ever take me seriously unless I lost fifty pounds and even then, my face could only get me so far. But, when I told Grammie she jumped for joy. She swore that was the career I was made for and she was happy that I was finally letting go of my fears to follow my dreams."

Trevor's whole body went stiff. What type of mother would say that to their own daughter? He fisted his hands trying to control his rage.

"Even though Grammie believed in me, every day I would have to fight against the odds to even be considered in any form of acting. I was kicked out of auditions, laughed at to my face, and even told to go open a restaurant instead by some asshole casting director..."

He would find that casting director and ruin his life. Trevor swore on it.

"Every time my mother would find out I didn't get the part, she would gladly throw it in my face." Maggie finally looked at him. "You reminded me of my mother."

Holy shit. No, no, no, the night was going so well. Ever

since the initial attempted brawl, there'd been no arguing, no trying to kill each other. But now, now—

"That was until you brought Pocket these cat toys. My mother never gave a shit about me or anything I loved. I don't even remember a time she bought me anything let alone clothes for school. That was always Grammie. My mother would have never bought me a necklace, especially one as beautiful as you did. And I know for a fact my mother would have tried to poison Pocket rather than buy him something to tell him he's loved..."

Wait, what?

"I hated you, Trevor. I hated everything you stood for, and the things you said to me. I *still* want to punch you in the throat for—"

"I'm sorry," he interrupted her. "I'm so sorry. You have no reason to ever forgive me, but please know I am truly sorry for the things I said to you and the way I treated you."

Maggie stared at him and for the first time, he saw her completely resigned. Almost as if she'd given up.

No. That couldn't happen. Her fire, her passion. It was why he fell for her to begin with.

"I moved here after Grammie died hoping I could make her proud that I was actually following my dreams."

"She would be proud of you," he said, desperately trying to figure out a way to fix this conversation and right his wrongs. He wasn't built for talks like this. And he sure as hell wasn't accustomed to them.

"No," she answered. "She wouldn't. The first part I'm cast in I almost get kicked off the set because I walked in on you and that bimbo. You then did everything in your power to get me banned from the set. You said some horrible things about me to my face, and then in the end, I foolishly slept with you. No, my Grammie would not be proud of me."

"Bullshit!" Trevor stood as he started to pace. "Your

grandma would be extremely proud of you. Hell, Maggie, not only have you been in a film here in L.A., which can I add most people spend their whole life trying to accomplish, you were also invited to one of the biggest Hollywood parties of the year. You've made some amazing friends and you are out there every day kicking ass. Your grandma would be so proud of you. *And,*" he spoke softly. "You've caught *my* eye."

Maggie laughed, narrowing her eyes at him. "Stop fucking with me, Trevor. I can only take so much before I snap. Besides I don't *need* your attention."

Trevor kinda like when she snapped, if he was being honest. "Hear me out. I'm not saying you should be lucky that I am giving you attention. Shit, no that's not what I am saying. Damnit. What I am trying to say is, I want you, Maggie. This is new for me too. I've never bought anyone jewelry other than my mother and I sure as shit haven't bought someone I'm interested in cat toys for their pet, but I'm trying. I know a relationship isn't about buying stuff for someone but... well, I guess what I'm trying to do and I'm obviously failing at is..." He stopped pacing as he looked at her with a heavy sigh. "I want you, Maggie. I want you for more than just one night."

Chapter Twenty

DID he want her for more than just one night? Trevor thought for a brief second after he declared his words. He'd never wanted someone for more than one night... At least until Maggie came into his life.

The more he thought about it, the more he liked it.

Trevor watched as Maggie's mouth opened slightly as her cheeks heated. That only made him want to kiss her more. Feel her lips against his, her body molded to his own.

Fuck yeah he wanted her for more than one night. He wanted her for all the nights.

As the thought raced through his mind, he shocked himself. Holy shit, he really did want this. He wanted all of this. Her, the crazy cat. Every last bit of it. And until his dying breath he'd do whatever he could to make up for the way he acted in the beginning. He'd never forgive himself, but he'd spend the rest of his life trying to fix it.

"I can't get enough of you," he growled low in his throat as his lips found hers in seconds as he overtook her mouth. Everything about her was mouthwatering, he didn't know if he'd ever tasted something so perfect before in his life.

More. He needed more.

He moved his hands to capture her cheeks in his palms, cradling her face, controlling their kiss.

"You're still a jerk."

She pulled herself away from him, making his heart sink. Was this what heartbreak felt like? Because fuck this hurt. Thankfully for him though, he only had a second to linger in that feeling before Maggie did the unexpected.

Thank fuck his reflexes were good. Trevor was able to catch Maggie with ease as she jumped into his arms, devouring his lips with hers. Trevor let out a moan that came deep within his throat as Maggie wrapped her legs around his waist.

Fuck yes. This is what he was missing. Someone that could spar with him, keep him on his toes, and completely give herself freely.

Maggie pulled away from his lips, panting. "I still think you're a pompous ass, and it might be all the talk about my family tonight, but I need this. I need you."

Beggars can't be choosers. And right now, even though he wanted more from her, he'd take whatever he could get.

Trevor pulled her closer to his body as he sought out her lips. He yanked her higher on his waist as he stood stumbling his way to her bedroom. "Fuck!" he stammered as they fell onto the bed. "How can your body feel this damn good?"

"Cushin' for the pushin'," she answered with a pant as she kissed his neck. "Now shut up and fuck me."

Trevor barked out a laugh as Maggie nibbled on his ear. Fuck, she was perfect. And, he was going to do whatever it took to prove to her that from here on out he was *her* man.

WHAT IN THE hell was she doing? *And freaking again.*

Maggie's mind wanted her to push Trevor off, but her

body refused. When he flipped them with ease so he was on top, her whole body shivered. No one had ever manhandled her like he did, and fuck if that didn't send a shockwave through her.

She needed to have a serious sit down with her body.

As Trevor kissed along her neck down the opening of her top, her heart raced. She wanted this.

She couldn't deny it, or him. Maybe it was his words, the fact she opened up, or maybe it was Lexi's voice in the back of her head telling her to go for it. Whatever it was, Maggie wanted it. Even if it was just for tonight.

"Baby, you feel so fucking good under me," he mumbled against her skin. "I need to feel more of you." Trevor grabbed the hem of her shirt and pulled it over her head, tossing it away from them. Any other time, Maggie would have fought to cover her body, but the look Trevor gave her, full of undeniable lust, stopped her.

"Up," he demanded as he hooked his thumbs over the waistband of her jeans. She did as he wanted and lifted her hips so he could pull her pants off. Once she felt the cold air hit her legs, it was if her nerve endings came to life all over again.

"What's this?"

Dazed, Maggie looked at him as his hand was in the front pocket of his jeans. Within seconds Trevor pulled out the necklace he'd given her.

She swallowed hard as he examined it, before he turned his attention back to her. Maggie was about to make some sort of excuse about keeping it on her when she saw his eyes darken.

It was like something snapped inside of him and a pure primal need took over as he pounced on her. His body came down on hers hard as he tried with all his might to mold them into one.

Maggie instinctively wrapped her legs around him. *Fuck*

yeah. With her emotions high, if Trevor wanted to be the predator and her the prey, she'd gladly take part.

"Don't worry, baby, I'm putting this where it's safe." Maggie was about to ask what he was talking about, but she then saw him place the necklace on the nightstand.

Seeing the sparkle of the pendant in the light ignited something inside of her. With all of her might, Maggie used her legs to flip them over, so Trevor was now on his back.

"Fuck yes," he growled as he moved his hands to her breasts. "You look perfect from down here." He quickly flicked open the front snap of her bra, making her breasts bounce free.

As Maggie looked down at Trevor, his eyes laser focused on her chest, she wanted more. She ripped at his shirt, demanding it to come off. Trevor effortlessly pulled her to him as he sat up removing the offending material and throwing it over her head toward the door. Maggie didn't know what came over her, but at this point, she didn't care.

All she wanted in this moment was to feel Trevor deep inside of her, and that's exactly what was going to happen.

THIS WAS the woman Trevor had fallen for. The feisty, take charge, doesn't take crap from anyone Maggie. She moved down his body hooking her fingers in his pants pulling them off in one swift move.

Holy shit, she was perfect.

Maggie peeled down his boxers causing his dick to spring forward. He could swear, the looks she gave it almost made him lose it right there. Without missing a beat, Maggie wrapped her fingers around the base of him, squeezing tightly, causing a hiss to escape his lips.

Fuck him, he was about to explode all over her face. And

as exciting as that sounded, he wanted to be inside of her first. Trevor was about to demand her to sink onto him when he felt the light touch of her tongue against the head. "Holy fuck!" He wasn't ready. His eyes rolled back into his skull as she enveloped him into her mouth. In all his life, he'd never felt something more perfect.

Too perfect in fact.

Trevor reached out with his hands to gently push her away when she decided to swallow. Instead of pushing, Trevor wrapped his fingers through her hair and prayed that he wouldn't embarrass himself. "Maggie, I can't..." he panted, as he gritted his teeth fighting his own body. "I can't hold on. I need to be *inside* of you."

"Then come get me." Maggie released him with a pop before playfully looking up at him.

He lost it. Within seconds Trevor had Maggie on her back, as he quickly ripped her panties from her body with one hand as he reached for the condom in his jeans with the other.

"You're mine." He looked her dead in the eyes as he thrust deeply inside of her.

"Yes!" Maggie's head hit the back of the pillow as she arched his back, as he moved inside of her. "More, please, more."

"You want more?" Trevor pulled out before thrusting back in with force. He lifted her legs to his shoulders as he maneuvered her for a better angle so he could work her fast and hard.

"Harder, Trevor." She looked at him, her cheeks were red and her eyes were filled with determination and lust. "I can handle it. Give it to me."

Maggie's words were enough to send him to the brink. Reaching between them he rubbed her clit as he thrust inside of her.

Fuck! Her walls tightened around him. She clawed at his arms as her orgasm rocked through her. As her walls clenched him harder, he lost all control. "Fuck!" he growled before stilling and spilling his seed deep inside her core.

Trevor froze as the world stopped around them while he tried to regain his breath. Holy shit. He didn't want this to end. He looked down at Maggie who'd closed her eyes as she breathed heavily. Panic suddenly shot through him, what if she asked him to leave again? He couldn't handle that a second time.

Not after this.

Just as he was about to freak out, to his complete surprise Maggie pulled on his back, causing him to collapse onto her. She then quickly rearranged them, so they were still intertwined. At first, he laid there motionless, afraid of what would come next. Then he felt Maggie curl into his body.

After a few moments with her not pulling away, Trevor finally let his body relax with relief. As he looked at her, a small smile spread across her face, which he knew matched his own. He leaned forward kissing her with as much passion as he did the first time.

This is exactly where he wanted to be and where he wanted to stay. He curled Maggie into his arms and within seconds she was fast asleep. Trevor was not far behind her, his body growing heavy from their exertion. However, before sleep overtook him, he glanced at the end of the bed when he saw movement out of the corner of his eye that caught his attention.

He was jolted awake once he realized he was looking directly at Maggie's cat.

Pocket stared him down.

At first, Trevor thought it was going to be okay, but then Pocket did the one thing that always creeped him out. He looked Trevor dead in the eye and slowly blinked.

Oh, shit.

Chapter Twenty-One

MAGGIE WOKE to the sensation of someone kissing the side of her neck. She was really going to need to work on her crazy dreams. It was bad enough she had slept with Trevor in the first place, now she was dreaming about doing it again. And here she was half awake imagining him about to fuck her once more.

"Finally." There was another kiss on her neck, causing her to open her eyes. "I've been trying to wake you for twenty minutes. I was about to go to drastic measures."

Maggie's eyes widened as the events of the previous night came rushing back to her. Nope, none of that was a dream. Trevor had shown up to her apartment, *brought Pocket cat toys,* and then put in a movie her and her Grammie used to watch.

Holy shit. And then they slept together.

Again.

"Trevor?" She swallowed hard.

"Who else would it be?" He pushed himself to the seated position resting on his elbows. Trevor looked over her shoulder down at her. When Maggie focused on his face, she pulled back. Why the hell did he look pissed? What was with this guy constantly running hot and cold?

"Who else spends the night in your bed?" He glared down at her as his nostrils flared.

What?

"Answer me, Maggie. Who else gets to see you like this?" His jaw tightened. "Do you let them touch you, *taste* you? Who is it? Who else is fucking you?"

Yep, Maggie somehow ended up on the crazy train again. She ended up boarded on that train a lot when Trevor was involved. As she watched his anger rise, Maggie couldn't stop herself, she burst into a fit of laughter.

"Maggie, this isn't funny," he growled, which made her laugh harder.

Bad choice on her part.

Within seconds Trevor was on her, straddling her waist. She screamed in surprise when he pinned her hands over her head. "Mine," he growled out, before kissing her hard.

Instantly, their tongues battled as he fought to control the kiss. "Mine," he reminded her as he removed his lips from hers and started kissing down her jawline. "Don't you fucking forget it."

A moan escaped Maggie's lips as Trevor kissed her jaw.

"Now that I have you, you're mine."

As her brain finally made sense of what Trevor was going on about, she jerked away from him. "Now that you *have* me? I'm *yours*? I am not an object to possess, Trevor."

"I possessed you pretty well last night. Just like I'm about to do right now." As he made his way to her chest, Maggie pushed him causing him to fall off her.

"What the hell!"

"You're an asshole." Maggie bunched the blanket around her body, holding onto it like her life depended on it.

"Not this shit again." Trevor righted himself, as an annoyed grunt escaped him.

Maggie was about to argue with him when her eyes darted to the appendage between his legs. Could you blame her? It was long, thick, and begged to be touched. And right now as it bounced around, she couldn't think straight.

"Eyes up here."

Maggie snapped her attention to Trevor's face. When she saw his smirk, she scolded herself for being caught. She quickly looked away. "Jerk."

"You keep calling me that." He laughed. "You're gonna give me a complex."

"What, that you *are* a jerk? Good."

"No," he mumbled before crawling up her body. "I think this is like the times when kids call their crushes mean names, but secretly they are trying to tell them they like them. Every time you call me a name, it just makes me feel all warm and fuzzy inside. You call me names a lot, so that must mean you like me a whole hell of a lot." He placed his hand over his heart and closed his eyes for a moment. "It brings joy to my soul."

Forgetting about the sheets, Maggie launched herself at him, knocking him onto his back. Straddling his waist, she pinned his arms above his head. "You are a fucking piece of work, Trevor McCain."

TREVOR WAS IN HEAVEN.

Absolute fucking heaven.

He *knew* he'd be able to get a rise out of Maggie if he pushed her hard enough. And, that was exactly what he wanted to do. The moment she woke up, he could tell she was overthinking again. And after last night, that was the last thing he wanted.

Looking at the woman above him completely naked set his world on fire. Her breasts swayed with her movements, her eyes gleaming with lust. The fact that she *thought* she could make him submit to her ignited him.

Sure, he could easily overthrow her, but why the hell would he want to?

All Trevor needed to do was lift her up a few inches and slide into her. He could already feel her wetness against his skin.

"Are you even listening to me?"

Was she speaking? "Huh?"

"Typical," she said before sliding off him and back onto the bed.

No! Come back!

Trevor pushed himself onto his elbows. His poor neglected erection swayed with his movements. *Don't worry you stupid bastard, I'll get her back.* "What are you going on about, Maggie?"

Sighing she grabbed the sheets and covered her body once again. All that did was piss Trevor off more.

Didn't she get he *needed* to see her body? He shot up grabbing the offending material and yanked it away. "How dare you cover up." Maggie looked at him as if he'd grown an extra head. *Good,* he thought, *hopefully now she'll finally get it.*

Narrowing her eyes, she reached for the blanket. "Give it back!"

"No." He tossed it behind them.

"Yes." She went to retrieve it, but he blocked her.

"Don't you get it? I *want* to be able to look at you at all times."

"I'll murder you."

"You and what army?"

As if on cue, Pocket jumped onto the bed right next to Maggie.

Oh shit!

Maggie looked at Pocket, and to his surprise, burst into laughter. "Pocket, I don't know what I did to deserve you but you are getting a freakin' steak tonight."

Pocket turned to Trevor and slowly blinked at him causing Trevor to shiver before moving to Maggie and caressing her chin with his head. He could hear Pocket's purr.

Weird ass creature.

"I guess those cat toys didn't win him over." Maggie laughed.

"I wasn't trying to win *him* over. Maggie, it's you. You're who I want." He shook his head.

She stopped petting Pocket and stared at him.

"I don't know how many times I am going to have to tell you, but it's true. Maggie Connolly, you are the one I want." He moved up the bed with his hand out to cautiously pet Pocket. When his fingers reached his fur, Pocket jumped from Maggie to him demanding more attention.

At least he didn't attack me this time.

"You keep saying that."

"I keep saying that because it's true. Yeah, we both know I fucked up. There is no denying that, but I want you. No," he corrected himself. "I *need* you."

They were both quiet as he continued to pet the cat. No arguing was good, right? At least for them, he thought so.

"I just don't understand," she finally said.

"What's there to understand?"

"Trevor, you were an asshole. It's still hard to wrap my head around the fact that you want to sleep with me, especially after the things you said."

He sighed as he placed his hand on his heart. "There you go calling me names again."

Maggie took the pillow from behind her and threw it at his face. "Jackass!"

"Exactly," he said. "Oh shit!" He braced himself as another pillow hit him. "Truce, truce!" He held his hands in surrender. He then pushed the pillows away and stared at her. She was beautiful. Her body was supple, her hips were the perfect size for his hands. Her hair was a mess, but it brought character to her face. Her cheeks were heated. Her breasts hung freely and if he looked a little farther south, he could see the beginning of her apex.

Everything about her was out of this world.

And, everything he never thought he wanted.

How hadn't he seen that the first day she walked in on him?

"You're right. I haven't given you any proof that I mean what I'm saying. Well, other than..." He looked down at his growing erection. He shrugged as he made it more visible.

He wasn't going to be embarrassed about what the sight of her body did to him.

"I want to prove it to you. I want to show you that I like you. I want to be with you, and..." He reached out to place a stray piece of hair behind her ear. "I know you have feelings for me too. Why else would you tell me everything you did last night? I want you to give us a chance to explore these feelings."

A WAR WAS RAGING inside of Maggie as the room fell silent. How could she believe him? But with the way he looked at her, how could she not?

Maggie looked down at her uncovered body. Her rolls were fully on display. Any other time she would have been mortified. But with the way Trevor looked at her, she felt anything but shame. All those vile words her mother and classmates had said would have danced through her mind, but this time they were seeming to disappear into the background.

Trevor seemed like he wanted her, but would he still want her as soon as the word got out? Would he stand by her side while people made fun of her or asked if he was doing it as a charity case? She wasn't anyone's charity case. She was Maggie Connolly and she wasn't going to take shit from anyone anymore. Her mother, her peers, and especially not Trevor McCain. "What about in public?"

"What about it?" He picked up Pocket and placed him between them so he could let the cat attack his fingers.

"You know," she whispered. "What happens when people find out you're dating the fat chick?"

Maggie instantly felt the room shift.

He glared at her. "If anyone, and I mean anyone, says anything about you, I will fucking rip out their throats," he growled. "No one says anything negative about you. *Ever.*"

"People will *always* say something negative about me, Trevor. It will never go away. *But* what will you do when they start saying negative things about *you* because you're with me?"

He cocked his eyebrow. "Like I give a flying fuck?"

Why did he have to look so attractive when he did that?

"Maggie, seriously, you should know by now I have never given a crap about what anyone says or thinks about me. That's not my style. And it's none of their fucking business. I'm not their fucking zoo animal."

"You say that now," she murmured.

"Where the hell is she?" Trevor snapped his attention around the room looking around as he pulled up the sheet looking under it.

"Who?"

"Maggie Connolly." He jumped from the bed and looked around the room, under the bed, behind the curtains. "I know for damn sure you're not her. The Maggie I *know* doesn't give a fuck what anyone thinks of her and will put anyone in their place. She fucking lives to spar. Now, where the hell is she?"

"Have you lost your mind?" She panicked when he opened her curtains all the way. Now his naked body was on full display in front of the window for anyone to see. Pulling him back she stood with her hands on her hips, her posture ready for a fight.

"There she is. Thank fucking God." He stepped closer to her before placing his hands on the sides of her face. He brought his lips down to hers.

"Come with me to the premiere, be my date." He kissed her again before pulling back to look into her eyes.

"Uhh, that's still a while away." Maggie worried her bottom lip as she looked at him.

"I know."

Chapter Twenty-Two

MAGGIE SIGHED HAPPILY as she took a deep breath of fresh air while she walked toward Perk You Up. It'd been a few weeks since she'd last made it to her friend's coffee shop, not for lack of trying though. Every time Maggie planned a trip to see Lexi, Trevor found a way to convince her otherwise.

She smiled as she walked along the pathway to the shop from Trevor's house. So much had changed since that night at her apartment. Sure, Trevor and her still fought, and fought a lot, but instead of storming off or trying to kill each other, they now ripped each other's clothes off.

Something she was *very* fond of.

The initial couple of days after their heart to heart were still awkward for her. Trevor kept surprising her. There were times she'd have random objects delivered to her. This included more cat toys, lingerie which she was not a fan of, even movies he thought she would like.

Which, if she were being honest with herself, she did enjoy. It warmed her heart with the effort Trevor was putting into their relationship.

Wait, was it a relationship?

Her smile widened as she realized exactly what this was. Yep, it was indeed a relationship. Although they hadn't gone out in public much, she couldn't deny they were in a full-blown relationship. Even though she was still getting used to it, there were aspects she was starting to like more and more.

Especially, the not sleeping alone.

Since that first night, Trevor refused to sleep without Maggie. Which was kind of sweet in a weird stalker way. If she insisted on sleeping at her apartment, which she did because of Pocket, or if they'd gotten into a fight, he'd show up at her front door after he wrapped for the day.

Sometimes with dinner or a movie in hand.

Along the way, he'd convinced her to give him a key, and Trevor took full advantage of it. Even though it seemed to be going fast there was something about it that felt right.

She reached for the pendant around her neck as she closed her eyes.

Happy.

She was happy.

Even when there were times he still annoyed the crap out of her. Like the nights he *demanded* she sleep at his place. She was happy. She didn't know when she truly forgave him for everything but it happened. And she was glad she did. Not once in her life had she felt this wanted and cared for before.

Her smile spread from ear to ear, and she had to laugh at his antics. Trevor was notorious for texting her letting her know he had *relocated* Pocket to his "second home" for the evening.

The first time it happened Maggie almost killed Trevor for stealing her cat while she was at the grocery store. But when she finally got to his house to take back her cat, seeing his arms all scratched up made it worth it. Was it wrong to laugh? Maybe. But it was sure as hell entertaining.

Now when Trevor *informed* her, he'd relocated Pocket,

she rolled her eyes and plotted to spike his food with laxatives. She would've put up more of a fight if Pocket didn't seem to love it at Trevor's.

Pocket, the devil cat himself, actually demanded to be there more than his *actual* home. Which made sense, there were more rooms for him to terrorize and cause havoc in.

But all that didn't matter, because being with Trevor felt right. It might have started out rough, but it felt right.

Walking the last few steps to Perk You Up, Maggie took a deep breath. She knew beyond a reasonable doubt, the second she opened the door hurricane Lexi was going to strike.

"You've finally come up for air, I see," Lexi remarked the second Maggie stepped inside.

"Good to see you too, Lex."

"I was gonna have a search party sent out for you." Lexi turned her back on Maggie. *Well, this was going well.*

"Lexi, I'm sorry, it's been—"

"I know, I know, you've been bangin' the life out of him." Lexi turned back and handed Maggie her drink.

"Is there poison in this?" Maggie looked at the cup then back at Lexi.

Lexi gave her a creepy smile, which caused Maggie to put the cup back down.

"Maggie, don't be silly. You'd know if I want to poison you. Now, am I annoyed that you've abandoned me..." She pointed to herself. "Your best friend? Yeah, but I also know you have a good reason to. I mean come on its Trevor freaking McCain. Not only would I abandon my friends, but I'd also sign away my first-born child."

"Oh geez, really, Lexi?" Maggie picked up the drink again and headed to the spot by the window.

"What? You can't blame a girl here." Lexi sat across from her with her own drink in her hand.

"Lexi," Maggie warned.

"Fine."

Lexi got up and pulled Maggie into her arms. "I've missed you. Our texts and random calls aren't good enough. I finally have a kick-ass best friend, then she ups and leaves me the second some guy drops to his knees for her... wait, scratch that. Can you tell me your secrets so I can have that, too?"

Maggie laughed. "I love you."

"Love you, too, kiddo. Now spill."

TREVOR SAT BACK in his chair as he looked over the last few lines he needed to record. Thankfully, all the filming had wrapped up. Now, all that was needed from him were some voice-overs and some dubbed lines.

"How's Maggie?" Danny came into the room and sat across from Trevor.

"She's good." He pushed his lines away from him as he looked at Danny. "I think she's finally heading over to Perk You Up this morning."

"Lexi's gonna enjoy that," Danny remarked. "She was telling me last night she was going to show up at your house and demand you let her best friend out for fresh air."

"It's not my fault Maggie can't get enough of me. I tell her all the time to go hang out with you two. She's the one that would rather spend the time in bed with me."

Danny cocked his brow.

"No, it's true. Sometimes I even beg her to go hang out with you guys. I need time to recover. But then she gives me those *fuck me eyes,* and I'm a goner."

"Bullshit." Danny laughed.

Trevor reached for the lines again avoiding Danny's glare. "Fine," he admitted, then he looked toward Danny giving him a smirk. "What can I say? I have *amazing* persuasive techniques."

Danny rolled his eyes. "Sure, you do."

Trevor laughed as a smiled appeared on his face.

"She's happy, though, right?"

"Yes, and I am going to make sure she stays that way," Trevor answered honestly.

"She doesn't deserve the shit she's gone through."

They both turned toward the door as Matt walked in. "I agree." Danny looked at his father.

"And I plan on doing everything I can in my power to make sure she never has to go through any of that again," Trevor added. "Fuck, man, I still beat myself up for the way I treated her. I don't understand why she even gave me a chance."

"I second that," Danny interjected.

"She gave you a chance 'cause like me, she sees the good in you. Yeah, you've been an asshole, we all know that, but deep down you're a good man," Matt said before taking a seat next to Danny.

Danny scoffed. "Sometimes."

All three of them laughed before the room settled again. "She's special," Trevor announced.

"We know," Matt agreed.

"I'm going to take her to the premiere as my date."

Danny and Matt both stared at him. "How does she feel about that?"

Trevor sat back in his chair. "I think sometimes she believes I won't really take her, or if I do it will ruin my career. But when that happens, I do everything I can do to prove to her I don't give a fuck what other people think of me. Slowly, she believes I do want to take her. Honestly, I can't wait to take her. Then everything will be out in the open and there is no way in hell she can deny my feelings for her."

"She still denies them?" Danny asked.

"She knows I like her and want to be with her. But she won't let go of her fears that our relationship will possibly be career suicide." Trevor fisted his hands. It was the one thing that they still truly fought over. He got it, he completely understood why she felt the way she did. She'd never had any sort of support system in her life other than her grandmother, and the things people used to say to her. Hell, if the roles were reversed, he would probably feel the same way. "I want to be with her. Fuck, I really lov—" Trevor cleared his throat. "She's who I want, and I will do whatever it takes for her to see that."

Danny stared Trevor down.

"I'm glad you finally found what you've been missing." Matt cleared his throat. "Don't hurt her."

"I won't."

With that, they both left, leaving Trevor to work on his script.

The words were running together as his mind tried to process what he'd almost said. He wasn't one hundred percent sure he knew what these feelings were, but he did know he wanted to explore them.

Trevor looked down at his watch. He only had one more set of lines to record, then he was done. He'd already told his agent to keep his schedule clear for a few weeks so he wouldn't have any distractions or obligations.

Trevor wanted time with Maggie and Maggie alone. The thought of her being in his bed every night sent shockwaves down his body. With a groan and a tug on his pants to make room, he looked at his lines again.

Just a few more hours, then he'd be able to go home to her.

Chapter Twenty-Three

MAGGIE LOOKED at herself in the mirror and glared at herself. How in the hell was she supposed to be "red carpet" ready? She still didn't understand what the hell that meant. She looked toward the makeup Lexi had brought her and narrowed her eyes at the offending objects.

"Babe, I don't think that's how you put on makeup." Trevor laughed as he made his way into the bathroom. When she turned her glare on him, he continued. "But then again, how would I know?" He came up behind her, encasing Maggie in his arms. As Trevor leaned in to kiss her neck, she couldn't help but melt.

Staring at their reflection in the mirror, she decided to push away her feelings of inadequacy and let the spirits of Trevor surround her. So many nights she still fought her demons when it came to Trevor, but slowly she was starting to embrace the new her.

Looking around the bathroom, she blushed. Over the past few weeks, more and more of her things had ended up in Trevor's home. She honestly couldn't even remember the last time they'd slept at her apartment. What scared her? The fact that she was starting to like this more and more.

Moving away from his embrace, she crossed her arms over her chest. "I'm still mad at you."

"When are you not?" He rolled his eyes reaching for his shaving cream.

"What's that supposed to mean?"

Trevor turned toward her, his brow cocked.

"Trevor," she warned.

"What? I didn't say anything." He went back to his task of shaving, dismissing her.

"Trevor freakin' McCain, do not make me hurt you." She tapped her toe with annoyance.

"Oh, baby, I would love to see you try." He put down his razor, washed off the shaving cream, and faced her. "Actually, I love it when you get all tough on me. It makes me hard."

"Trevor..." she growled.

"Fuck yeah, Mags, say my name."

He reached to pull her to him, but she stepped back. "No, you big bully. I'm pissed at you. How could you have junked my car *without* even talking to me about it?"

"Not this again." Trevor crossed his own arms over his chest. "I did you a favor."

"You did *me* a favor?" Her eyebrows shot up.

"Yeah." He winked her way. "Better yet, you should be on your knees thanking me."

Does this man have a death wish? Her right eye started twitching.

"I mean it, Maggie. You should be thanking me. We both know that car was a death trap. It needed to be done. I just went ahead and did it."

"Without even asking me!" she shouted. Sure, she knew her car wasn't very safe, but nonetheless, it was *her* car. She had worked really hard to get it and without even a second thought he'd sold it.

Trevor growled.

Then she heard Pocket voice his opinion from the other room. Why in the hell was Pocket *always* taking Trevor's side now? That thought added more fire to her. Not only had he come in and started controlling her life, he now stole Pocket's loyalties as well. "Don't you growl at me, mister," she snapped, turning her attention back to Trevor.

"Or what?"

Pocket screeched again. *You've got to be kidding me!*

"I'm waiting..." He advanced on her, making her body shiver. She still didn't get why this was her favorite part. "I think you *knew* the car needed to be junked and you're just picking a fight because you're angry about having to get ready tonight for the premiere."

Well damn.

He had her number. Sure, she did need to replace the car and she was upset about it. She knew he did it for her safety. He was right, though. She was stressed and angry about tonight. This would be the first time since they started officially dating that they would be going to a huge event *together.* Yeah, they'd been seen around town but there hadn't been many rumors. After tonight though, everyone would know— that is if he still wanted people to know.

Maggie clenched her fists. She needed to stop doing that.

Trevor pulled her into his arms. In one fell swoop, Maggie was lifted onto the counter, her towel ripped from her body. "How many times do I have to tell you, you'll never have to worry about anything?" he mumbled into her neck as he began to pepper kisses along her skin.

What were words again? She tried to say something, but her body had other plans. *Stupid sex-crazed body!* He made an inaudible sound.

"In about three hours, I have a whole team coming here to help you. Hair, makeup, the works."

She pushed away from his body to look at him. "How? What? Why?"

Trevor chuckled before moving in to kiss her chin. "I knew you've been stressing about this. I also knew you didn't want to bother Lexi with it because she's busy getting ready on her own. So, I arranged for a stylist team to come here and take care of it for you." He went to kiss her, but she held out her palms pushing against his chest. The shock was apparent on her face and she could feel it.

Maggie continued staring at him as it finally hit her.

This was the moment she realized she loved him.

She shouldn't have been surprised, but here she was. The feeling almost drowned her. She grabbed the back of his head pulling her lips to his. Opening her legs, she wrapped them around his waist, pulling him closer to her. Her body continued to grow hot as she felt Trevor's member press into her wet folds through his jeans. "Please," she begged.

This moment consumed her soul, and she knew she wouldn't be able to live if she didn't connect herself with him and now.

Love. Love. Love.

Maggie freaking loved him. *Holy shit.*

"Now," she pleaded as she tore her lips from his and started kissing along his jawline.

"You know I always give you what you need." Trevor dropped to his knees throwing her left leg over his shoulder. Before she could comprehend the change in positions, Trevor had opened her and started to feast. Her hands instantly went to his hair as she rode his tongue.

She'd never get tired of this.

"Now," he demanded. "Come now."

Normally she was all for defiance when it came to Trevor

giving orders, but this time she willingly gave in. As her orgasm washed over her, she shook. Holy crap on a cracker. As she fought to catch her breath, she looked down at the man between her thighs. *This is the man I love with my whole heart.*

Trevor quickly stood as he unbuckled his pants. Shoving them down to his knees he positioned himself at her entrance. Maggie locked her legs behind him, as she urged him to move forward.

"You're mine," he growled before slamming into her.

Always.

TREVOR FELT something shift as he entered her. Their sex had always been hot, but he could feel the difference this time. He pulled out of her and looked into her eyes. And, for the first time, he could swear he saw into her soul.

Instead of freaking out, it only encouraged him to make their connection more intense. As he moved inside of her, he brought her face to his, as he demanded her mouth.

More.

He needed more.

Reaching his hands behind her, he grabbed onto her ass, bringing her body closer to his.

"Yes," she moaned.

Trevor's passion overtook him as he lifted her off the counter and into the air. Her panic at his actions caused him to trip on his pants that were still around his knees and lose balance. Before he knew it, they were both on the bathroom floor. Not caring about the pain that shot through his body he held onto her hips, keeping her firmly in place.

"Oh, shit, Trev, are you okay?" She tried to move off him, but he stopped her. "As long as I'm still inside of you, I will *always* be okay." With his declaration, he shot his hips up and continued to move inside of her. "Fuck me, Mags. Fuck me like you've never fucked me before."

"Oh, God," she moaned as he took control of her body, bouncing upwards into her core.

Trevor felt his release building, but he refused to let go before she did, though. "Give it to me," he growled. A few more strokes and he felt her body clench around his.

"Yes!" she screamed as her orgasm took control of her. He slammed into her one last time before stilling. Maggie instantly collapsed on top of him.

Trevor crashed his head onto the bathroom floor trying to catch his breath. *Holy fuck.* This was how he wanted to spend the rest of his life. Panting, he placed his hand in Maggie's hair. There was absolutely nothing that could ruin this moment.

"Owwie," Maggie yelled before sitting upon his chest. Wait? What he hell? Was she hurt?

"Damnit, Pocket!"

Trevor looked behind Maggie and saw Pocket was doing what Pocket did best. As the cat continued to attack her toes, Maggie jumped off him. Trevor looked down at his feet where Pocket was now eyeing him. With one slow blink, Pocket focused his attention on the appendage that was half erect.

"Fuck!"

Chapter Twenty-Four

TREVOR SAT IMPATIENTLY AS he waited for
Maggie to come out of the bedroom. As soon as the team he'd
hired showed up, they'd whisked her away and shut him and
Pocket out of the room. He'd been ready to go to the premiere
for at least an hour now. And, there was no telling how much
longer Maggie was going to take.

Trevor absentmindedly reached out to pet Pocket on the
back of his head. Instantly, he was rewarded the only way
Pocket knew how.

"Damn it." He pulled his hand away to look at the
damage. "You better be glad I love your mom or you'd be
outside before you could do that creepy ass blink."

"Are you fighting with Pocket again?" *Oh shit, had she
heard?*

Trevor shot his head to her and froze. It didn't matter if
she heard because there in front of him Maggie stood in all her
glory. She was beautiful in her everyday clothes, but this, this
was off the charts. She was in a skin-tight forest green dress. It
showed off an hourglass figure that should have been illegal.

Her hair was in loose waves, pushed all to one side. Her

makeup was classic Hollywood pin-up. As she moved closer to him, he saw the pendant around her neck fully on display.

His heart stopped.

Fuck he loved this woman.

He really loved her.

Trevor took a deep breath trying to remember how to speak. Damn he loved everything about her. His body was more alive than ever before. All he wanted to do was throw her over his shoulder, toss her onto the nearest flat surface and rip that dress off her. *Holy shit.*

"Pocket got your tongue?"

Maggie's voice jarred him out of his thought. A thought he wanted to relive over and over again. He cleared his throat as he looked her up and down. "You look so beautiful."

Her smile was wider than he'd ever seen. As he looked down her body, he stopped at her feet and burst out into a deep laugh.

"Hey!" Maggie slapped his arm.

"Only you would wear flats." He chuckled before pulling her into his arms.

"They wouldn't let me wear my Converse, so flats were the compromise."

"Just so you know, you're perfect." He pulled her in for a kiss.

MAGGIE SAT NERVOUSLY NEXT to Trevor in the back of the limousine.

This was it.

The second they stepped out of the vehicle the whole world would know they were together. This could be career suicide for him. Looking at Trevor, she felt her reservations come back full force. "Are you sure about this, Trevor?"

Cocking his head he looked at her. "Sure about what?"

"This."

His eyes sparkled. "I've never been more sure about anything in my life." He grabbed her hand and squeezed, his action instantly calming her. If he wanted this, then who was she to stop him. She sat back in her seat as she brought his hand to her chest. "It's your funeral."

"Why you little..." He jumped on top of her. He kissed her like she'd never been kissed.

Before they knew it, their driver had announced their arrival. Pushing Trevor off herself, she did her best to fix her hair. "Oh, shoot, do I look okay?"

"You look so good I could fuck you right here in front of everyone."

"Trevor," she warned. "I'm being serious."

"So am I."

She growled. "Did you mess up my hair or makeup while you took it upon yourself to grope me?"

He smirked while her eyes narrowed.

"Trevor."

"You look fine, baby." He took her hand before grabbing the door handle. "Are you ready?"

Maggie looked past him where she could see all the people waiting. Their cameras at the ready. Was she ready for this? She felt Trevor squeeze her hand again. "I'm as ready as I'll ever be," she finally answered.

Once they were out of the limo, instantly bright flashes were all around them. Voices were on top of one another. *"Trevor, who's she?" "Trevor, over here!" "Who's on your arm tonight? She looks a little different than your normal type." "Trevor, is she your latest bed bunny?"*

The noise all started to meld together. Oh God... She felt her palms start to sweat as her insides quaked. Why the hell had she decided to do this?

"She's kinda fat..."

"Excuse me?" Trevor abruptly stopped causing Maggie to fall into him. *Oh no! Universe, do not do this to me!*

"What did you say?" Trevor repeated, looking directly at the paparazzi asshole.

"Nothin' man. Just stating the obvious."

Trevor cocked his head to the side as if to say, *oh really?* "Good to know. Stating and doing the obvious is what I'm all about." He reached out and grabbed the guy's camera before smashing it onto the ground. He then turned to someone behind them. "Get the guy a new camera, one model better than this one. But, before you give it to him, make sure he understands if he *ever* fucking says shit about her again that camera will be shoved up his ass." With that, Trevor started walking again pulling Maggie along.

Maggie was mortified.

"Don't worry about them. Pay them no attention."

She stared at him shocked. "Are you fucking kidding me? Trevor, you just destroyed that guy's camera and then *threatened* him in front of everyone. And all for what? Because he said something about me? Newsflash, Trevor, that happens on an everyday basis to me."

"It fucking does?" He stopped walking and turned toward her. "Who the fuck said anything about you? Tell me their names now and I will end them."

"Oh, for the love of—"

"Tell me, Maggie. No one disrespects you and lives to see another day."

Maggie rolled her eyes, but inside she was screaming for joy. Not only did he take her to the premiere, he publicly stood up for her. What a stupid man.

But he was her stupid man. "Don't get your panties in a twist." She chuckled trying to defuse the situation. "Let's just get inside and go find Danny and Lexi."

"This isn't over." Trevor eyed her, but gave in.

"No," she agreed. "It's not. But, for right now it is. Plus, I just want to get inside, watch the film and head to the after party, then go."

"And, here I thought you *never* wanted to party." He leaned in kissing her as she heard the camera shutters all around her.

Well, if you can't beat them, you might as well join them. She pulled Trevor by his suit jacket and kissed him with all her might.

THE MOVIE WAS PHENOMENAL. Maggie was so proud of Trevor and all he'd done. He brought his character to life like no one else could. It was one of the reasons everyone wanted to work with him in Hollywood.

And, then there was watching herself on the big screen. When her part came on, she could swear her heart had stopped. She was able to relive every moment and she loved it. This was the reason she wanted to become an actor to begin with. She was on the edge of her seat the whole time as she watched the movie. Sure, she'd hear some comments here and there about her and Trevor, but when she looked back at him, his eyes were never on the screen. Instead, they were on her. She held his hand tightly as they walked into the reception. Sure, *all* eyes were on them and there was an endless amount of questions being flung at them. But, somehow, Lexi and Danny had taken it upon themselves to intervene and block all of them.

Maggie laughed as she watched a press agent make a beeline toward her and Trevor. Before Maggie could open her mouth, Lexi was there, throwing her arm over the press agent's shoulders and steering them away.

Tomorrow she was sending Lexi and Danny a candy basket!

Trevor pulled her into his side as they made their way over to Matt.

"Matt." Trevor nodded once they were next to him.

Maggie smiled. She was so overjoyed with how the night had turned out. It was perfect.

"Hey, you two. Seems as though you both are the talk of the town." Matt laughed.

"Let 'em." Trevor grabbed a stuffed mushroom off Matt's plate, popping it into his mouth.

"Hey!" Matt pulled his plate from Trevor's grasp causing Maggie to laugh. With one quick maneuver, Trevor was able to steal the morsel and pop that into his mouth too.

"Jerk." Matt placed his plate as far away from Trevor as he could. Matt quickly scanned the party then nodded in the direction of the refreshments. "What do you think is going on between those two?"

Maggie glanced to where Matt was referring to. Her curiosity getting the better of her, she saw Danny with his arm wrapped around Lexi's shoulders.

"They'll get there," Trevor said.

"You think so?" Matt asked.

"I do," Maggie chimed in, beaming as she looked at her two best friends. She truly believed they would.

Removing her gaze from her friends, she looked back at Trevor. This night had been perfect. Even though she was being stared at more than she'd ever been in her life, nothing could ruin it. Not even the thought of the trash magazines and what they were going to say tomorrow.

Sighing, she put her arm around Trevor's waist. Looking at him, she realized he'd been staring at her. His eyes gleaming with joy. "You looked beautiful on the big screen," he whispered in her ear.

Maggie's heart swelled.

"You've got a strong career ahead of you."

"I agree," Matt said. "I actually wanted to talk to you about this role I think would be perfect for you." Maggie's eyes nearly popped out of her head.

Yup, tonight was perfect.

"Trevor, baby," Maggie heard a sultry voice from behind her. Turning to the sound she came face to face with the one woman she never wanted to see again.

Within seconds, Maggie was thrust back to that first day she'd met Trevor when she walked in on him and *this* woman.

"Baby," she said again finally getting Trevor's attention.

Trevor turned. His face paled. "Fuck me."

Chapter Twenty-Five

TREVOR FELT Maggie stiffen in his arms causing him to look toward her. Instantly, his stomach bottomed out. There standing a foot from him was the woman he'd been screwing when Maggie had walked in. "Fuck me."

"Anytime, baby," she purred.

What the fuck was her name?

Maggie pulled her arm from around Trevor's waist and started to slink away from him. "Excuse me," she whispered. *Fuck!*

The woman, fuck, he couldn't even remember her name. As he looked this woman up and down, he actually recoiled. Why in the hell had he ever thought she was attractive? Her hair was bleached so bad the strands looked like they'd been burnt. Her nose job was hideous, and there was nothing to her. He could probably push her over if he blew a little too hard. There was absolutely *nothing* about this woman that attracted him.

"Where have you been, babe? I've been wondering when I'd see you again." She moved closer to him.

As she reached out to touch his chest, Trevor grabbed her wrist. "Don't," he growled, his tone dangerous.

"What, babe?" She actually laughed at him. "Did you forget how fun we can be together?"

"Don't touch me. Don't ever touch me."

"Trevor..."

When he looked to see who called his name, he saw Maggie. Her eyes were wide and her cheeks red. She was embarrassed. Fuck. That pissed him off even more. Seeing her like that was as good as a knife to his stomach.

"Trevor, please, you're making a scene."

He was making a scene? Hell yeah, he was about to make a fucking scene.

"Oh Lord, aren't you the girl that walked in on us, you know the fat one?"

Maggie's face paled as she stepped back and into the chest of Danny who'd come up to them. Danny instantly put his arm around her. That only pissed Trevor off even more.

Fuck. He was going to lose it. When Maggie was upset, she should come to him, no one else.

"You are that girl! Isn't this wonderful, I can't believe they actually let you in here. Aren't they afraid you're gonna eat all the food?" The bitch laughed reaching out for Trevor again.

The shrill voice snapped his attention back to her. Did this woman have a death wish?

Trevor steeped away from her. "Watch your fucking mouth."

The woman's eyes widened. "Excuse me?"

"You heard me, you bleached blond leathered skin whore. If you say one more thing about her, I'll make your life a living hell." Out of the corner of his eyes Trevor could see the crowd forming around them. He didn't care though.

The woman crossed her arms over her chest and straightened herself. Her eyes narrowed on him as she spoke. "Oh, now isn't this just wonderful." The woman looked at Maggie and then to him. "What is this some publicity stunt? Be nice to the fat chick so you can get better press. Believe me, Trevor, no one will ever believe it's anything more than that."

"It's everything more than that," he snapped. "Why don't you get your bony ass out of my face before I make sure you'll never step foot on another movie set in your life."

The woman's jaw dropped. "You can't do that!"

"Try me."

"He might not be able to, but I can." Matt stepped up from behind him.

The woman glared at both of them before reaching for the drink that was on the table and throwing it in Trevor's face. "Have fun porking the pig, you egotistical jerk."

Trevor took a step after her but was held back by Matt. "Don't do it. I'll make some calls tomorrow. She'll never get another decent job in Hollywood again. I'll make sure of it."

"That's not good enough!"

"Think of Maggie." That's what got Trevor to stop fighting against Matt. When he scanned the crowd, he saw Maggie in the arms of Lexi and Danny, clearly trying to make herself invisible. That only pissed him off more. Seeing her again in Danny's arms sent a new wave of possessiveness through him.

"Get your hands off of her," Trevor yelled before pulling Maggie to him. The heat of the moment had pushed him to the brink. "You don't touch what's mine. Ever!"

He snapped his attention back to Maggie. Her cheeks were red and her eyes wide with embarrassment.

Putting her hands on his chest, she pushed him back, before she turned to walk back to Lexi and Danny. "Can you guys take me home?"

"You've got to be fucking kidding me." Trevor grabbed her arm pulling Maggie back to him again. "Why do you always have to fight me? Jesus, Maggie, how many times do I have to tell you? You're mine."

"You're a pig. Stop making this worse."

Trevor rolled his eyes. It was her favorite insult to sling at him. "I get it, you're embarrassed and pissed right now. If I'd known she was even on the guest list I would have asked Matt to take her off. But fuck, Maggie, when you get upset you need to come to me, not run into the arms of another man."

"He's my best friend! And you were being a hothead!"

"I was defending you. Why are you so ungrateful?"

Maggie stared directly at him, her hands were on her hips and her brow raised. "Excuse me, did you just say I'm ungrateful?"

That's it. He'd had it. Trevor mirrored her stance. "Yes, you're so fucking ungrateful. I fucking paid for your piece of shit car when it broke. I then bought you a *new* car. I pay for your apartment that you're not even living in because I moved all of your shit into my house. I let your cat beat the shit out of me every chance he wants to because it's a game to him. I arranged for you to have a stylist and—"

"I never wanted any of that stuff. You did it all on your own. I am and was perfectly happy with the way everything in my life was going. You came in and decided you needed to be in charge." She moved a step closer to him. "You did all those things behind my back. Yeah, I'm glad you did do those things, but you make it seem like I need to bow down to you for sticking up for me. Newsflash honey, I can stick up for myself!"

"Do you think I don't know that!" he yelled. "Maggie, I do all those things because I'm fucking in love with you!"

Everyone froze as the room fell silent.

Fuck it, he didn't give a shit. It was about time he told her. Hell, he'd fucking yell it from the rooftops if that's what it took.

"What?" she whispered.

"You heard me, Maggie. I am unbelievably in love with you. You are the biggest pain in my ass, but you are *my* pain in the ass. And..." He took a deep breath. Might as well go for broke. He kneeled down on one knee. "Fuck, I can't believe I am going to do this here. Maggie, you set my world on fire. You are constantly keeping me on my toes. I know this is all a lot to take in, but I can't see my life without you. You're it for me. And, until the day I die, I will still buy you a new car when I want to keep you safe or pay for a stupid bill you insist on having, like as a wasted apartment. I want to pay for all of Pocket's vet bills and hopefully get him a brother or sister..." He narrowed his eyes at her. "...but it'll be a dog and I'm naming it. Maggie, here's the thing you need to know, I will *never* stop defending you. You are my dream girl and I will fight for you every fucking day."

Maggie had her hands over her mouth as she took a cautious step forward, tears threatening to fall from her eyes. "Wh-why are you on your knee?"

He moved his head to the side and cocked his eyebrow. "Really, you don't know why I am on my knee right now?" Shaking his head, Trevor grabbed her hand. "Maggie, I am asking you to marry me. Right here, right now. This is it for me. You're it. I want you to be my wife."

"Holy shit..."

"If you say yes, keep in mind I will never stop trying to surprise you. I will never stop defending you, and I will never stop loving you."

"Don't leave the man hanging. Jump his bones!" Lexi yelled from somewhere in the distance.

"Lexi!" Maggie shot her head to her friend. "Do *not* ruin the moment I tell the man I love I am going to marry him!"

Trevor jumped to his feet scooping Maggie into his arms. "So, that's a yes?" he asked, spinning her around.

"Yes, you big oaf now put me down!"

"Hell no." He spun them again. "I'm never letting you go."

"What if I told you I'm going to be sick?" That got him to stop spinning her. Trevor carefully placed her on the ground cupping her cheeks in his hands. "I love you, Maggie Connolly. You're my Hollywood dream come to life."

"I love you, too, Trevor. Even though I want to kill you half the time. I somehow fell so madly in love with you." She pulled away punching him in the arm. "Don't ruin it!"

Trevor laughed before pulling her into his arms once more.

The crowd around them erupted in celebration.

"Let's go home." Trevor kissed her again.

Maggie nodded and they started to make their way out of the party as camera lights flashed all around them.

However, they both stopped the moment Lexi stood in front of them, blocking their path. After pulling Maggie into a hug and releasing her, she looked her up and down. "You get twenty-four hours before I come over and we start planning the wedding."

"Oh crap!" Maggie's eyes widened as she looked at Trevor.

Chapter Twenty-Six

MAGGIE FOLLOWED behind Trevor as they ran up the steps of his home. Well her home now, too, she guessed. This was all still a little too surreal for her, but she was ecstatic, nonetheless.

"Devil cat, I mean Pocket," Trevor yelled as he opened the front door. "Your Mommy and Daddy have a surprise for you."

"Trevor." Maggie laughed as she followed him.

"But we really do."

Pocket, always knowing when he is being talked to, came out from around the corner and sat down in the hallway looking at them. With one slow blink, he yawned, clearly waiting for the news that took him away from what she presumed was his cat nap.

"There you are." Trevor walked over to him. "Guess what, big guy? Your Mommy and Daddy are getting married."

Another slow blink from Pocket. "Well, don't act all excited." Maggie rolled her eyes, before moving to Pocket to pat the top of his head, earning her another slow blink. "The cat never shuts up, and the second we actually want to talk to him he's quiet."

In protest, Pocket opened his mouth wide and bellowed.

"There's my boy!" Trevor scratched Pocket under the chin. Trevor then turned toward Maggie, his eyes showing nothing but pure love at her.

Maggie stood there trying to remember how she even got to this point. So much had happened, things she hated and things she loved. She'd met some amazing people, followed her dreams and now she was standing in front of the man she once had a crush on and then hated. But now, she didn't think she could go one day without loving him.

Trevor must have felt the same since he took two steps and cupped Maggie's cheeks in his hands. "I love you, Maggie." He kissed her. Kissed her like a man that was drowning and was finally getting air. After a moment he pulled away, kissing her nose. "My fiancée."

"I guess so." Her smile went from ear to ear. *Holy crapolie. I'm going to marry Trevor. Freakin. McCain! Whoa, wait a minute, that's actually kinda scary...*

"No," he growled, snapping her out of her thoughts. "Hell no, get whatever thought you just had out of your head."

She cocked her brow as her hands went to her hips. "And, how do you know what I was thinking?"

"Are you kidding me? Do you really think I don't know you? It's written all over your face." Trevor pulled her into his arms. "Let me remind you. I love you and only you."

"That's a nice thing to say."

Trevor barked out a laugh. "How did I get so lucky?"

"Who said you were going to get lucky?"

Trevor effortlessly lifted her, making Maggie wrap her legs around his waist or she'd fall. "I know I'm getting lucky. You hate when I'm not buried deep inside of you." He let out a growl. "But in all honesty. I love you, Maggie. You're who I want to spend the rest of my life with. You. And only you."

Maggie's heart skipped. God, he was such a pain in her ass, but when he said things like that, she couldn't help but melt. "I love you too, you big buffoon."

"Who are you callin' a buffoon?"

"You."

Trevor laughed before taking her mouth with his. One thing was for sure, there would never be a dull moment between them. And Maggie wouldn't want it any other way.

They made their way into the bedroom. Trevor tossed her onto the bed, climbing on top of her.

Man, she would never get tired of this.

As Trevor kissed his way down her neck, he palmed her chest. "God, I love this dress. Too bad it's not going to last another second."

"No!"

It was too late. Trevor had ripped the beautiful dress right down the middle. "I'm gonna kill you. I loved this dress!"

"I'll buy you another one." He continued kissing his way down her body. He looked into her eyes as he dipped his tongue into her belly button. "How is it you taste better and better every time?"

"They put some marshmallow body lotion on me."

Trevor's tongue was off of her in an instant as he shot up. "*Who* put it on you?"

Maggie rolled her eyes as she did her best not to sit up and slap him upside his head. "The people you hired to help me get ready tonight."

"They touched you?" Trevor jumped off the bed as he went for his phone.

"Drop it right now mister, or so help me."

Trevor glared at her. "How could you let them touch you? Better yet, why would you?"

"Oh, for the love of all things. No one touched me you, you Neanderthal. They handed it to me and told me to make sure I put plenty of lotion on. I misspoke." He crossed his arms over his chest, clearly deciding if he wanted to believe her or not.

Maggie sighed as her head fell back onto the pillow. Nope. There would never be a boring day married to Trevor.

Doing the only thing she could to distract him, Maggie sat up, before she slid her hands down her body pulling her panties off.

That did the trick.

"Mine!" Instantly, Trevor was on the bed ripping her panties off her body. *Thought so.*

"Damn, you are so beautiful and all *mine.*" Trevor tore his dress shirt off sending buttons flying through the room. Which then caused a certain cat to start chasing after them, informing everyone within earshot the second he caught one.

Maggie threw her head back and laughed as Trevor removed his belt from his pants. Yup, this was the life she was going to live, and she wouldn't want it any other way.

Chapter Twenty-Seven

THREE WEEKS LATER

"**FUCK**, how do you always feel this good?" Trevor growled as he pushed himself inside of Maggie. He'd only started to pump inside of her and he could already feel his climax taking over. How in the hell did she always do that?

He looked at her hand and saw the engagement ring he'd bought her the day after he proposed. It glistened as it hit the sunshine from their window. He still couldn't believe he was actually going to be marrying the woman of his dreams. And, in less than a few months at that. He loved that she proudly wore his ring. Even at auditions. His eyes quickly shot to the pile of wedding magazines that were on the floor by the bed. Lexi had clearly taken the "maid of honor" duties to the extreme. Something he was trying to get used to. Danny wasn't pushing his way into all the planning and he was the best man.

Damn, he still couldn't believe he'd asked Danny to stand next to him. But honestly, he couldn't see it any other way. They had gotten pretty close as the weeks went on. Everything was falling into place.

"Once you go fat you never go back." *What the fuck did she just say?*

Trevor slapped her ass. "If you ever say that again, I promise you won't sit for a week."

Maggie turned to look at him over her shoulder at him. "And, I'll sic Pocket on you."

He glared at her, pulling all the way out of her core.

"What, no! Get back here, you moody bastard." She pushed her hips back but didn't move since Trevor held her tight in place.

Trevor then flipped over and sat on the edge of the bed, crossing his arms over his chest. He glanced down at his dick that was now protesting its sudden absence of a perfectly wet, warm hug.

"Trevor, don't make me hurt you." Maggie jumped from her position on all fours and stood in front of him.

"Stop saying shit like that about yourself."

"I was only joking." Maggie lowered herself to her knees. "Besides, I know you love me just the way I am." She gently grabbed his dick, stroking him lightly.

Trevor tried to suppress the sensation running through his body but was failing miserably. Her hot little hand moving up and down his member made him lose all coherent thought. Before she could take him into her mouth, though, he turned his body. "I will *not* let you use me."

"Oh, for the love of the universe." She looked at the ceiling. "Why did you give me a man that has worse mood swings than teenage girls on their periods?"

"I'm not moody," Trevor scoffed, glaring at her. "I just hate when you talk crap about yourself." To him, she was by far the most beautiful creature he'd ever laid eyes on. Especially right now, when the only thing she had on was the necklace he bought her all those months ago and her engagement ring.

Sighing, Maggie took a deep breath. "I'm sorry, Trev. I

didn't mean it. Honestly, I was just joking. It was a dumb thing to say. Do you forgive me?" She batted her eyelashes and moved her body slightly so her breasts would sway.

Damn, she was a master at this. "You're forgiven." He pulled her into his arms. "Don't do it again, though." He tossed her onto the bed with a squeal of excitement from her. Climbing between her legs he positioned himself at her entrance. Maggie instantly arched her back accepting him.

The second he was fully inside of her, Trevor lost it. "Marry me?"

"Dummy, what do you think this is?" Maggie held up her left hand showing him the ring before dropping it and moaning when he hit her spot.

"Damn straight you are." Trevor moved faster inside of her. Fuck he loved this.

He was about to explode when he heard Pocket take his famous running jump into their bedroom door. The cat hated being locked out of a room and would do anything to fight his way inside.

"Not again," Maggie groaned.

"Ignore him." Trevor moved inside of her, slowly building to where they were.

Damn, he loved this woman. He loved everything about her. How he originally thought she was anything but perfect was beyond him.

Maggie really was *his* Hollywood dream come to life, and he'd spend the rest of his life proving that to her.

"We need to get him a friend. Someone he can play with instead of trying to screw with us."

"Really?" Trevor's brows shot up as he stopped moving. "You want to talk about this now?"

Maggie innocently looked at him, her cheeks red. "I guess this isn't a good time."

He rolled his hips causing another moan to escape from her, as he smirked. "Ya think?"

"No, you're right," she agreed. "Right now, I want you deep inside of me."

Trevor couldn't argue with that. He thrust inside her making sure to hit her spot every time he moved. Within minutes, he felt his body tighten as he found himself on the edge. As Maggie's walls clenched around him, he only needed to push one more time—

"I'm here! Come on, Mags, we got lots of wedding planning to do!"

"You've got to be fucking kidding me!" Trevor yelled as he looked down at Maggie.

"Uh... Maybe I shouldn't have given Lexi a key."

Maggie was going to be the death of him. He thought about it for a quick second and then shrugged. "Fuck it!" Wedding planning was just going to have to wait.

THANK you for reading Hollywood Dreams. I hope you enjoyed it.

Do you want to read about a very opinionated Corgi, his accident prone mom, Holly and her Adonis veterinarian husband, Ben?

If so check out their story in Stumbling Into Him.

Look for a sneak peek on the next page.

Stumbling Into Him

CHAPTER ONE

"WATCH OUT!"

Holly Flanagan heard a commotion coming from the other side of the park.

Figuring it was best to ignore the shouting, she bent over to focus on picking up her Corgi—Lord Waffles's—most recent deposit. Although, with Holly's track record, she should've known anyone yelling "watch out," "take cover," or "that's about to fall" was directed at her. Even after years of being the unofficial spokesperson for unlucky, klutzy, and clumsy, she still ignored the shouting as she carried on with her dog parent duties.

Unfortunately, for her before she could register what happened, she was knocked onto her back with pain radiating from her mouth and nose.

"Well, at least the sky is pretty today," Holly mumbled as she tried to get her bearings. Looking away from the sky, she reached for her mouth as the pain spread.

"Miss, I'm so sorry. Are you okay?"

With a heavy sigh, Holly closed her eyes.

Was she okay? Wasn't that the million-dollar question?

She'd just been hit with something and she was pretty sure some part of her face—she didn't know which part—was bleeding. Waffles hadn't stopped barking, and her head hurt.

So, was she okay?

Holly groaned with a heavier sigh escaping her lips.

Yeah, she was fine. This was just another normal day in her life. And so far, if being hit by an unknown projectile to the face was the worst thing that happened to her, she would considered it a good day.

Deciding to face the music, she opened her eyes.

Holy shit!

Above Holly, only a few inches from her face, was by far the most handsome man she'd ever laid eyes on.

He should be on the cover of a magazine hot. He had dark brown hair and deep blue eyes that were richer than the ocean. His jaw was chiseled, with a light dusting of scruff—in the alpha male, I'm in charge here kind of way.

Wonderful. Freaking wonderful...Okay, let's add embarrassing yourself in front of a Greek God to your list of accomplishments for the day. Hey, it can only get better from here, right?

When Holly realized she'd been staring at him for what might have been considered too long, she quickly jerked her head forward, trying to right herself. Sadly, for her, though, she slammed her head right into the guy's forehead.

Really!

Great. Not only did her mouth hurt, now her head hurt... and well, let's not forget she'd just head-butted the hottest man in the world.

Absolutely freaking wonderful!

"Shit," the Greek God grunted.

Slowly, Holly opened her eyes only to see her Adonis holding his head. *Great. Could today get any worse?*

As if the Universe heard her, Waffles barked loudly in her

face, looked at the pile still on the ground, and then back at her.

"For the love of all things, dog. I was about to pick it up," she growled. As she took her hand away from her mouth to deal with his majesty, *Lord* Waffles, she screamed when she saw blood on her hand.

"Oh shit. Lady, you're bleeding." The man grabbed her chin moving it from side to side as he examined her face.

"Oh, God, what happened?" As she looked at the blood, her heart raced. *Did I break my nose? Wait, am I unconscious? Am I dying? I'm dead right and to add salt to my wound I'm greeted with the hottest man alive?*

The man tilted Holly's chin back to get a better look. "I was tossing the Frisbee with Ripley and it somehow veered off course. I tried to warn you when I yelled *watch out.*"

Typical. Holly groaned. *Hot guy throws a Frisbee. Said Frisbee hits me in the face. Hot guy then insinuates it's my fault for not getting out of the way fast enough. I mean, I know I'm generally invisible to men like him, but, damn. You'd think these extra wide hips would make me be seen.* Her eyes darted to the Frisbee sitting next to her as she glared at it. *I don't know why, but I'm blaming you.*

With one last huff directed at the Frisbee, she glanced back at the man.

"I can't tell if it's just a busted lip or worse," he remarked while he tilted her chin upward even further.

That's it. This was already embarrassing enough.

Holly ripped her face from his hand. She'd be able to tell if it was only a busted lip. She'd had them more than enough to count in her life—from falling down, objects to the face, and even falling *up* the stairs a few times. She reached into her pocket and pulled out the napkin she had stuffed in there to wipe her mouth.

"Let me see," the man demanded, as he took the napkin from her and dabbed it on her lips.

In an instant her eyes widened as she froze.

Well, Holly. This is the most action you've had in months. And, if some hot guy is all over you, you might as well enjoy it while it lasts.

As the man inspected her lip, Waffles crawled onto her lap and started kissing the underside of her jaw, demanding attention.

Holly rolled her eyes. *Great. Thanks, Waffles, for bringing the attention of my double chin to McHotPants.*

"Thanks for trying to help me clean up your mom," the man remarked before quickly abandoning his job of cleaning the blood off her mouth to scratch Waffles on the head.

"He's not trying to help you," Holly grunted. "He's *trying* to remind me I still need to pick up his poop and give him a treat."

"Shouldn't your mom be the one getting the treat if *she's* the one picking up your shit?" The handsome man cocked his head at her dog.

Waffles, ever the one to argue, looked at the man—who now had a mischievous grin on his face—with the most judgmental side-eye he could muster.

No one came between him and his treats.

With a small chuckle he ignored Waffles's glare, and gave him another quick scratch, this time under his chin, before moving back to Holly's mouth dismissing the dog. "I think it's just a busted lip, but your front tooth..." The man coughed as he sheepishly looked away.

"My front tooth?!" Holly ran her tongue along the front of her teeth. *Fuck!* The jagged piece was unmistakable. "Crap." She quickly pulled her phone from her pocket and launched the front-facing camera. As soon as she saw herself, she jerked back.

Holy shitballs. Her hair was all over the place, her face was red, and there was still blood on her...

Well, you've definitely had better days, Holly. She took a deep breath before he hastily opened her mouth to see the damage.

"Oh, no..."

Staring back at her was a chipped front tooth, the damage matching her busted lip. *Wonderful. Absolutely wonderful. Thank you, Universe. Thank you so freaking very much.* She didn't know whether to laugh or cry. *Clumsy Holly strikes again.*

As her eyes flooded with tears, a cold nose hit her arm. Realizing it wasn't Waffles since he was still in her lap, Holly looked to her left and saw one of the most beautiful gray and black Australian Shepherds she'd ever seen.

"Aren't you a cutie?" Everything going on was instantly forgotten as her love of animals overrode everything.

"That's Ripley." The Greek God chuckled, his eyes twinkling in a way Holly thought was only possible in movies. "I'd thought you'd be more concerned about your mouth than a dog?"

"Well you don't know me." Ignoring him, she reached out to scratch Ripley's chin. "You're so pretty. Aren't you?" Ripley must have agreed, because she barked once before kissing Holly's hand.

"Uhh, miss? I'm not a human doctor, but I think we should pay more attention to your injuries instead of the dogs."

"Human doctor?" Holly snapped her head to him with her right brow cocked. "As opposed to what, an alien doctor?"

"I haven't worked on any aliens that I know of, but I did neuter a cat named Alien once. Does that count?"

Holly's eyes widened. "You have got to be kidding me? Of course you've got a body of a Greek God, and are also a vet.

Which means you love animals. *Freakin'* wonderful. You're like the most perfect guy and here I am on the sidewalk with blood pouring out of my face with a chipped tooth and a pile of poop a few feet from me." She pushed Waffles off her lap and stood. "Please excuse me while I find a place to die of embarrassment."

"You're funny." The corner of the sexy man's mouth quirked upward.

"And you're hot. So, we've now successfully established which groups we belong to." Annoyed at herself more than anything, she angrily started to stomp away from him.

"Hey, wait up!"

She spun around to glare at him. It was his fault she was in this mess to begin with. It was his dumb Frisbee. However, the moment Holly saw Waffles sitting at the foot of the man looking up at him, her left eye began to twitch.

Of course, her dog would betray her. She wouldn't expect anything less from him. "Waffles, come." She gently pulled on the leash, but the dog wouldn't budge. "Lord Waffles, get your butt over here."

The man cocked his brow. "Lord Waffles?"

"Yeah," she answered. "He thinks he's a freakin' king. Hence the 'lord' and I love waffles. Do you got a problem with that, buster?"

The man burst out laughing as he scratched Waffles on the back. To make matters worse, her betraying Corgi rolled over asking for belly rubs.

The audacity! That's it. No more treats for you! She glared at her dog.

"Who's a good boy?" the man cooed. "You've got a weird name, but you're the best boy, aren't you?"

Holly's eye twitched harder.

As she stomped back toward her bastard of a dog, but out of nowhere, her foot hit an invisible rock causing her to trip.

Within a split second, she ended up falling right into the arms of the bane of her existence at the moment.

"Whoa, are you okay?"

"I'm fine," she grumbled as she righted herself. *Go ahead and add this to the, "it can only happen to me" list.*

"I feel like you need to walk around with a warning sign or at least a crash helmet."

"Not the first time I've heard that." Quickly she bent down and scooped Waffles into her arms. "If you'll excuse me. Not only do I really need to find a secluded place to die of embarrassment, I also need to call my dentist or go to the walk-in clinic. Maybe both." She turned on her heel and began power walking down the sidewalk.

The moment Holly passed the spot she'd tripped at, she examined the cement coming up empty. Figures, there'd be absolutely nothing there. If there were a sporting category on tripping over invisible objects, she'd win gold every time.

"Hey!"

Holly kept walking doing her best to hide her humiliation while ignoring the Greek God who now chased after her.

"Hey, I want to make sure you really are okay." He caught up to her in two point three seconds.

Stupid short legs! "I'm fine."

"Your lip's still bleeding."

She glared at him. "Thanks for the heads up."

"Hey..." He reached for her arm stopping her next attempted escape.

"What?" she snapped.

"Let me help you. My practice is only a block from here. I've got all the supplies to clean up your lip and I can get a better look at your tooth."

"You're a vet." Her eye twitched again. *Could today seriously get any worse?*

"I'm pretty sure if I can surgically remove nuts from an

animal I can look at your busted lip." He shrugged, sending her a smirk.

Crap on a cracker, he does have a point. He'd at least be able to see if anything was really bad. But no. She shook her head. This was already too embarrassing and she really didn't need to add this to her list. "Thank you for the offer—"

"Ben," he cut her off. "My name's Ben Richman." He held out his hand, which Holly stared at like it was her mortal enemy.

"Thanks for the offer, Doctor Richman, but there's a walk-in clinic not far from where I live."

"Please call me Ben. And let me do this. Trust me, you'd be doing me a favor."

"How would I be doing you a favor?"

"I'll be able to sleep tonight knowing the woman I maimed with my Frisbee is somewhat okay."

Holly watched as his eyes pleaded with her. In her arms, even Waffles—the jerk—looked up at her and whined. "Oh, for the love of... fine. Lead the way, *Ben.*"

"Thank you." His mouth curved into a smile. "Follow me."

When Ben whistled, Ripley sat instantly by his side as he bent down and fastened her leash before walking toward the street.

Holly stood there for a second and looked at the man and then back at Waffles who was clearly enjoying being carried. "Guess you get an extra trip to the vet."

She burst out into a deep laugh when Waffles closed his mouth and glared at her.

*Continue Ben & Holly's story in **Stumbling Into Him...***

Check out the Fun Facts on the next page and where to find me!

About the Author

Molly O'Hare is a USA Today bestselling author of plus sized/curvy romance books.

She's obsessed with all things animals, mainly Corgis, and body positivity. She grew up with severe dyslexia: trust her, spelling is not her strong suit. Over the years, she's become a huge advocate of "just because you learn something a little differently than others doesn't make you less." To help herself fall asleep, she'd create stories in her head, always picking up where she left off the night before. Molly figured if she got enjoyment out of her imagination, others might as well. So here we are.

Stay Connected

Sign up for my newsletter or check out my website.

Fun Facts:
I adore every animal I come across.
I read non-stop.
I have a cat just like Pocket in this book, but he's worse.
I believe in body positivity.
I love to cook... and eat.
I prefer to laugh more than anything else in the world.
Oh, and I want to own a sheep.

www.ingramcontent.com/pod-product-compliance
Lightning Source LLC
Chambersburg PA
CBHW061616100726

47898CB00002B/686